MARS

MARS

Stories by Asja Bakić
Translated by Jennifer Zoble
Afterword by Ellen Elias-Bursać

FEMINIST
PRESS
AT THE CITY UNIVERSITY
OF NEW YORK
NEW YORK CITY

Published in 2019 by the Feminist Press
at the City University of New York
The Graduate Center
365 Fifth Avenue, Suite 5406
New York, NY 10016

feministpress.org

First Feminist Press edition 2019

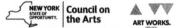

This book was made possible thanks to a grant from New York State Council
on the Arts with the support of Governor Andrew M. Cuomo and the New York
State Legislature.

This book is supported in part by an award from the National Endowment
for the Arts.

This book is published with financial support by the Republic of Croatia's
Ministry of Culture.

First printing March 2019

Cover and text design by Suki Boynton
Cover image © 2011 by Bruce Ritchie

Library of Congress Cataloging-in-Publication Data
Names: Bakić, Asja, 1982- author. | Zoble, Jennifer, translator.
Title: Mars : stories / by Asja Bakić ; translated by Jennifer Zoble.
Description: New York : Feminist Press, 2019.
Identifiers: LCCN 2018011671 (print) | LCCN 2018022322 (ebook) | ISBN
    9781936932498 (ebook) | ISBN 9781936932481 (trade pbk.)
Classification: LCC PG1420.12.A345 (ebook) | LCC PG1420.12.A345 A2 2019
    (print) | DDC 891.8/3936--dc23
LC record available at https://lccn.loc.gov/2018011671

CONTENTS

MARS

DAY TRIP TO DURMITOR

The secretaries explained first that a dead person's soul goes wherever she'd expected to go.

"Everyone wants to go to heaven," I said. "It must be too crowded there."

"It's not," said one of them. "Most people are so unimaginative that they simply stay wedged in the ground, like a potato."

"So I was lucky?"

"You weren't made for the soil."

"Wait a second," I interjected. "I can't tell the two of you apart."

"I am Tristesa," said the one on the left.

"I am Zubrowka," said the other.

"Like the vodka?"

"Listen, kiddo, don't complain," she said. "You drink what you poured."

Death is typically a European film. The scenes are evocative, the atmosphere and characters charged. But in my case, death took on a different form. I suppose my final moments spent in front of the

TV determined it. I was watching *Rambo* and unwittingly took his motto, "Alone against everyone," to the world beyond. *If it worked for him, it probably will for me too* was my first thought once I realized what had happened. It wasn't clear where death's pervasive melancholy had gone: with the two secretaries who could only be distinguished by the color of their underwear (Tristesa's were blue, to match her mood; Zubrowka's, pink), it wasn't realistic to expect the New Wave or anything like that.

"Where's God?" I asked.

Zubrowka smiled and said that God didn't exist.

"He must be somewhere," I insisted.

"You should've been more careful when you had the chance. You can't champion atheism and then play cards with the Lord when you die."

When I was alive, I'd written a funny play about a sex-obsessed God and his gay disciples. If nothing else, I figured, this place would be like that. It wasn't like I hadn't considered Him.

"God slipped in the tub," Zubrowka said after a moment.

I didn't believe her. It was obvious from the way she kept looking at Tristesa that they were up to something.

"You can't keep things from me and use my heathenism as an excuse."

The secretaries shrugged and offered up more reasons. Seeing that I'd learn nothing from them, I gave up my line of questioning.

To be honest, I just didn't think God was necessary; I was used to getting along without Him. And the secretaries weren't any more necessary. I couldn't figure out where they'd come from. At first I thought I'd lifted them from some comic strip I'd read long ago, but as time passed (I'm using the word *time* reflexively, because death doesn't free the brain from such useless signposts), it became clear that they weren't under my control. The secretaries came with death. This was, needless to say, frustrating.

I was trying desperately to understand. I couldn't shake the feeling that my head was slowly expanding from all that strain. This whole time, I thought, it had been growing on all sides. It was right in front of my nose, but I hadn't noticed it. Actually, it wasn't right in front of my nose because it was my head, and, however big it was, I couldn't see it without a mirror. Tristesa was rubbing her hands together in a satisfied manner. It was plain on her face that she was attentively following the growth of my head and was quite pleased. She called over Zubrowka.

"She's thinking?" Zubrowka asked as if I weren't in the room.

Then she looked at me and patted me on the shoulder. "This is just the beginning. We have an idea for how to make it grow even faster."

"But I don't want an enormous head," I said nervously.

"The head doesn't ask," said Tristesa. "It simply grows."

At that moment, I regretted choosing *this* instead of the potato option.

The secretaries had a clear plan. My head had become some sort of expensive egg. It resembled, in their words, one of those luxury Easter eggs from Czar Nicholas II. Since I didn't have a mirror, I had no other choice but to believe them. The question was, What did they think they'd find inside?

"Stories, loads of stories," said Zubrowka. "That's why you're here. We want you to write a whole book of them. If we like it, we'll let you proceed to the second phase."

"Second phase?" I asked.

I clutched my head. It didn't seem to be growing, but still felt unpleasantly distended. I began to stroke my hair fretfully, panicked at the thought that in the second phase I'd discover only my skull had been growing, while my brain had stayed the same size.

I wasn't sure if I had anything to do with it, but suddenly, not knowing how, I found myself in a hallway straight out of a fairy tale: *There are many doors you can enter, except for the last one, blah blah blah.* Of course, I wanted to see what was going on in that last room because, when I was alive, I'd watched a TV show about the difference between stupid and smart children. Scientists had conducted an experiment on a group of kids; they'd left them alone in a room with a two-way mirror they used to observe them. Before leaving a child, the scientists would warn them not to, under any circumstances, look at what was hidden under a white sheet on the table. The children who peeked were the smart ones. The others—not so much. Only one child turned out to be stupid, though. And not only was he stupid, he was also fat. I didn't want to be him. If it weren't for my desire to know, the size of my head would be a paradox. I bravely reached for the doorknob, but it was, of course, locked.

Where does a woman go, if she doesn't know what's in store for her? I was plagued by questions. I'd wondered a great deal in life too, but in death the questions that confronted me were harder, and the feeling of false finality was driving me crazy. The secretaries laughed loudly behind the locked door. They were obviously having fun, like they were reading something hilarious.

"Why are you named Tristesa?" I asked when they suddenly appeared behind me. "I've never seen you sad. You're always laughing and having a good time."

"You should've learned by now that you can't trust death, or people."

"We should go," said Zubrowka, pulling Tristesa by the sleeve. "She needs to continue."

Alone once again, I watched the door close. I wanted to run after them, to join in their merriment, but I couldn't move. My head was throbbing, and I felt like at any second it might explode—the *big bang*. I walked once along the hallway, up and down, but quickly grew tired. I opened the door to the nearest room, took a seat at the table that happened to be there, and began to write. But as soon as I put my pen to paper, I knew I had to write about writing, and that was dangerous because it wasn't what I'd been brought here to do. I needed action, events—that was clearly what the secretaries preferred. Death is like a dream where you're running, headless: you don't have time to stop and reflect because that would mean you've awoken, and in my case that just wasn't possible. I'd never heard of anyone waking up from death.

What to write about then? Everyone tends to write autobiography, which I find repulsive. But while I was feeling judgmental, a memory surfaced of my grandmother, how she would raise her legs and massage them, one after the other, while my sister and I watched, in awe of her calloused heels. Everyone wants to read autobiography, so give them autobiography—it can even be fictionalized. Why should the secretaries be any different? Death loves other people. It's not concerned solely with itself. It collects names, faces, human destinies, and gladly reads them. Fine, I thought, I will write about myself. And throw in a little about them; let everything be saccharine and romanticized, in the pastel shades of their underwear. But when I got down to writing, it became clear that I didn't know how to write sappy stories. I wrote how I thought, and my thoughts were explosive.

When I was six years old, I fell off the kitchen counter and landed on my right hand, breaking it. At the emergency room, I sat next to a little girl with a bandaged leg. She said she'd been playing with an ax and the blade had fallen right on her foot. I never complained again about pain. Pain became superfluous to me; it was reserved for others.

I remember well enough the apartment I grew up in—it was a two-bedroom apartment on the thirteenth floor. The elevator never worked so we always had to use the stairs. I shared a room with my sister, who once stopped talking to me because she found my writing "gross." I was hurt at the time, but she was right. My writing really was gross. I was a disobedient child and I stayed that way: mischievous through and through.

Every night when my family would fall asleep, I'd go out on the balcony and watch the parking lot, imagining morbid things, like a black van carrying off little children to some unknown place. I'd tell myself that soon it would be coming for me. Such vile things excited me, but I never ate my own boogers. To me, that was truly disgusting. Whenever I saw a child eating their own boogers, I'd smack them on the head.

I remember vividly my first grade school trip to Ozren, a mountain in northern Bosnia and Herzegovina. In the evening we'd lie in absolute darkness. I don't remember how many of us were in the cabin, but all the girls would scream for the teacher when, just as everyone was on the edge of sleep, I'd tell scary stories about witches and monsters. *Look at that woman lurking at the window*, I'd say. I often forgot how timid other children could be. The only thing that had frightened me was the dentist, and I'd quickly gotten over it. I returned from Ozren another child, one who wouldn't stop talking. My family dubbed me the Philosopher. I was always waving my hands, gesticulating wildly. I wrote poetry with a carpenter's pencil. I was truly special. I was different.

"You don't seem that different to me," said Zubrowka.

She leaned over my story, tapping her finger on the word *special*.

"It's only a story," I said.

"I know, but you shouldn't think so highly of yourself. You're not the first to sit at this table and write."

"At *this* table?"

"Yes, at this table," said Tristesa, who was standing on the other side.

"Exactly how many people have sat at this table before me?" I asked.

"We can't tell you, it's confidential."

I was confused. If I'd invented such a death for myself, how could it have been the same for those before me?

"I don't get it," I said. "You told me that it was potatoes in the ground or whatever, but really, it's either potatoes or this?" I paused, then added, "Is this heaven . . . or hell?"

Zubrowka and Tristesa gave each other a knowing look.

"It depends on the person," Zubrowka said. "For people who don't know how to write, this is hell. For those who love it and know how to do it well, this is heaven."

"I beg to differ."

I rose from the table and crumpled up my story.

"I want to go back in the ground," I said.

"Impossible," Tristesa replied. "First the stories, then you can proceed."

"Proceed where exactly?" I asked, once again nervous.

"We can't tell you, it's confidential," they said in unison.

I began to walk around the table. Tristesa reached for me.

"Get your hands off me! Don't you dare!" I yelled.

The two of them backed away toward the door, not taking their eyes off me. Once they'd left, I straightened the crumpled paper and copied the beginning of the story onto another sheet. I needed to keep going, needed to bring death to its conclusion.

To be honest, I wasn't actually special. I had an eccentric personality, sure, but plenty of others did too. I wasn't unique.

Before taking this thought further, I paused. The secretaries' second phase was tormenting me. It sounded like they were planning on robbing a bank or overthrowing the government, and I was supposed to help them somehow. I chuckled to myself and wrote: *Writing isn't an explosive. It can't blow up a safe, a wall, or a basement.*

"You're wrong," I imagined Tristesa correcting

me. "We said we needed loads of stories because we need enough to light the fireworks."

"I don't want to participate in anything illegal," I said aloud, as if talking to Tristesa.

"Fool!" she shouted, ending our imaginary argument.

I kept writing.

After he had an accident, my uncle came to live with us. Mama took care of him. He slept in the living room for a few months. At night, I'd watch porn right next to his pillow and laugh. I knew he didn't hear me. He had a good excuse—he was sick. The rest of the family was healthy and no one paid attention to me anyway. Of all the kids at school, I was the most invisible. Or it seemed that way, at least. I went to school alone, I came home alone. I didn't have any friends, just an immense desire to know everything.

As it happened, I did have one friend, an imaginary one—a unicorn named Sebastian who would only appear when I had a fever. I refused to go to the hospital, because one time there I'd spoken to the wrong people about him. They'd started to think I was crazy. My sister had saved me at the last minute, and together we'd escaped.

"If it weren't for you freaks," Zubrowka had said earlier, "every death would be a potato."

My back was beginning to hurt; I needed to stretch my legs. I stepped out into the corridor and walked toward the room at the end of the hall. I didn't hear the two secretaries giggling, so I assumed they'd gone outside somewhere. I tried the doorknob again: still locked. And then—who knows where I got the courage—I decided to break the door down. I kicked it a few times and managed to get inside.

The room was full of cardboard boxes, stacked all the way to the ceiling. In the middle was a table with two chairs and a small lamp. I guessed this was where Tristesa and Zubrowka sat. I opened one of the boxes at random and saw it contained manuscripts.

"What are you doing?" I heard Zubrowka's angry voice.

"It was open," I lied.

"She destroyed the door," said Tristesa, picking up the broken bolt from the carpet.

"I needed to know."

"We would've told you soon enough, if you'd just been a little more patient."

"I couldn't. The second phase is torturing me."

The secretaries sat down at the table. Since there weren't three chairs, I had to stand. Tristesa turned on the lamp and a weak glow lit her gloomy face. But their irritation didn't last—Tristesa began to laugh and bang her fist on the table.

"So you needed to know!" she said.

She laughed loudly, as if her mouth were full of other people's laughter—as if she'd stuffed herself with it like cake.

"I like you," she began. "I know Zubrowka likes you too, so I'll tell you everything. Here's the deal: we

13

gather the most interesting posthumous texts, light a big ceremonial fire, throw the paper in it, and . . ."

She paused and raised her hands in the air to heighten the tension.

"BOOM!" she shouted. "All the best there is in death will emerge into the light of day."

"You mean, the dead will walk among the living?" I asked, confused.

"Not all the dead, only the ones who write well."

Zubrowka, who'd been sitting in silence, spoke up.

"Literature is," she said, "the primary link between life and death."

It seemed to me that they both glorified writing too much, but I didn't want to interrupt.

"We need the heat of the written word to open a small rift so we can step into reality. You've read fairy tales, you know how it works."

"But fairy tales are made up," I said.

"Fairy tales are, but death isn't. There's no fucking around with death," said Tristesa. "Death reaches even the most inaccessible places, but only through literature. Otherwise death can do nothing."

"And the other arts? What about painting, sculpture, music?"

"Those don't interest us," they said. "They can, of course, be of use, but writing excites us more."

I closed my eyes. I imagined my unicorn friend Sebastian.

"Do you hear what these two morons are saying?" I asked him.

"I hear, I hear," he whinnied. "Remember Heraclitus. When people die, they're confronted by what they didn't expect or consider. Count to fifty to calm down."

"I've forgotten numbers," I said. "I can only count to ten."

When I opened my eyes, Tristesa and Zubrowka showed me one of their boxes.

"This is where we put the most valuable manuscripts."

"Who wrote them?" I asked.

"That's a secret," Zubrowka said. "But you'll know when we return to the living."

"Now you must keep writing," said Tristesa. "We don't have much time. The necessary condition for our departure is a total solar eclipse."

"That, or a full moon," added Zubrowka. "Really, it's all the same. There just needs to be some element of horror."

"Okay," I said.

I left the room, and in the hallway I started to think that, compared to the idiocy the two secretaries had described, a bank robbery wouldn't be all that bad.

Gold is worth more than life, I thought.

How did I know this? I knew because at one time I'd been alive and witnessed it myself. But I needed to stop all my theorizing. The secretaries wanted to resurrect me, to bring me with them. I honestly didn't feel a strong desire to breathe air again and see what was happening on the other side, but this idea about the power of literature had completely possessed me. Everything I'd written—two tiny books of poetry that no one read anymore—had ended up in local libraries. Writing that collected dust versus writing that resurrected the dead—there was no doubt about which I could get behind.

I wrote day and night, nonstop. Tristesa and Zubrowka brought me food and drink, and periodically wiped the sweat from my brow. Thirty days later the moment of truth came. They sat at the table and read what I'd written. They glanced over conjunctions and pronouns, laughing all the while.

"This is it!" they exclaimed. "Time for us to get going."

They jammed my manuscript into a box, secured it with duct tape, and placed it off to the side. I craned my neck to see if they had placed it in the "most valuable" box, but that one was already closed. As if all the best literature had already been written in the past, long before me. I found this annoying. Two tiny books of poetry, okay, but they were still significant. No matter their size.

"Go into one of the rooms," said Zubrowka. "You're not allowed to leave until you feel a force, like a lasso, pulling you toward the door."

"Okay."

I holed up in the same room I'd been writing in. The chair was uncomfortable, but so was my life.

And my death was uncomfortable too. I was used to discomfort.

A great heat spread through the room, and I thought I might be burned alive along with my posthumous brainchild. I sat still, not expecting that what the secretaries had described would literally happen—but then I felt something tightening around my waist, binding my hands to my body and pulling me toward the door.

My friend Sebastian appeared.

"We're going back among the living," I said. "Can you believe it?"

"Heraclitus says that immortals are mortal, and mortals immortal, because the life of one is the death of the other, and the death of one is the life of the other."

"Enough already with your Heraclitus!" I snapped.

Sebastian regarded me with an offended look.

"What a goose you are. How I wish I could've been Heraclitus's imaginary friend instead of yours. You have no appreciation for delicacy. From an airplane one can see you're from Bosnia."

Before I could respond, the door opened and I was sucked into the dark of the hallway. Above me spread blackness. I had no idea where I was. It seemed like I was emerging from a bottomless abyss.

"Where are we?" I asked the person next to me. I couldn't see faces in the dark.

"I think we're in Montenegro," said a woman's voice.

Once my head was out, I looked around. I'd never been to Montenegro.

"Durmitor," someone called out.

I was in the water. I saw Tristesa.

"Where are we?" I asked.

"Devil's Lake," she said, laughing.

A full moon shone down on us. I looked at my reflection on the lake's surface. Naturally, I was a zombie. No one returns from death undamaged.

"You could've warned me," I said to Tristesa.

"Why do you think zombies devour human *brains?*" she said. "It's not like writers spend their lives obsessing over genitals or feet."

She was right, of course. The great invasion of undead writers began its hunt for the human brain. Everyone hurried to get out of the water. Somewhere ahead of me I spied the poet Njegoš.

He would no doubt get the honor of the first bite, I thought, frustrated.

Even the zombies, unfortunately, practiced etiquette and respected the hierarchy. I tried to make a fist, but my hand didn't cooperate. The lasso still held me tight. Who was tugging the rope, who was steering me toward someone else's brain—I never managed to find out.

BURIED TREASURE

I.

The dead man was still lying there; tomorrow the mortician would come for him. In the meantime, they tried to calm his widow, a seasoned pill-popper, but soon gave up—the usual amount of drugs wasn't working, and she flailed on the bed, visibly distressed.

"Give her a larger dose," the doctor said.

The nurse read between the lines and gave her a fistful of pills. The widow then asked to be put in bed next to her deceased husband; she felt she was lying next to a living person. The grandchildren ran in and out of the room, ignoring their grandmother. Sometimes they'd pause to touch the corpse.

"Maybe he's really alive," the eldest granddaughter said.

The sour smell of the dead man's urine emanated from the bedpan.

The adults mourned, each in their own way, but the children had no time for grief. At that moment they were just beginning to discover sex, which, had the parents known, would've devastated them more than the grandfather's death.

The children didn't care that the things Grandpa had left behind were meant for adults. They converted each of them into something useful: his books became a staircase for dolls, his medals were turned into coasters. But the fate of some wooden pencils he'd kept in a drawer was most interesting. Not long after his death, the eldest granddaughter came upon her cousin crouched behind one of the couches, poking at her genitals inquisitively with one of the pencils. Though the eldest was hardly surprised, she decided this tarnished pencil could no longer be used for writing or drawing. Furthermore, if her cousin had used *one* pencil in this way, perhaps she'd used the rest of them for her private fun as well. So part of Grandpa's inheritance ended up in the trash. The parents weren't pleased—thinking that the girls had thrown them away carelessly, they demanded the pencils be salvaged and returned to circulation. The children said nothing, even when someone in the household would anxiously nibble the end of a pencil while composing an important letter.

Once Grandma had recovered, she promptly returned to her old routines. She still hid pills in her underwear drawer, furtively stashed food among her winter hats, and let the children watch *Twin Peaks*, despite the fact that their parents had expressly forbidden it.

In a rapid acceleration of their childhood, the grandchildren had learned about their grandfather's scrotum when it had peeked through the leg of his briefs. But the funniest thing they'd ever seen was two floors down in the apartment of Nataša, a neighbor whose father was a big fan of pornography. A few visits to her place, and Grandfather's "shame" was completely forgotten.

Nataša's father collected erotic comics and magazines, and she had a wooden horse the children would all take turns rocking on, in order to simulate the sexual activities of adults. They were quickly found out, and the entire porn collection ended up in an empty parking lot, tossed from the car like money to the poor from some affluent balcony. Nataša's mother thereby ended a very pleasant spring, the likes of which they'd never experience again. Despite this, the children continued to observe strange things, things that made *Twin Peaks* look like no big deal. They became especially attuned to secrets. Everything that was hidden, the children wanted to unearth. They couldn't stand whenever the adults would lie, even though they themselves lied gratuitously. But the most important thing was that they were still naive. If they hadn't been, nothing that happened that summer would have been possible.

When Grandma finally stopped crying for Grandpa and stockpiling trash and pills around the house, the children set off with her and their uncle for summer holidays in Smoluća, the village where Grandma had been born and raised. When they arrived, Uncle immediately relocated from the driver's seat to a bench under a walnut tree, opened a beer, and gazed at the hillside in front of the cottage. The children, three young girls desperate to know everything, surrounded him. Uncle took big gulps.

"Will you take a bath in a barrel later?" asked the children.

"Of course," said Uncle.

Their cousins were supposed to arrive at the neighboring cottage the same day. As soon as they got there, everyone would climb trees and pelt each other with unripe fruit, especially plums. Uncle would help them draw thin, twisted mustaches on their faces. They'd steal corn from the nearby fields and blame the village children. The eldest cousin would probably eat too much of the green fruit and corn and, just like last year, spend two hours holed up in the outhouse. The children would laugh and laugh, offering her a fresh roll of toilet paper along with their disgust. Everything would be business as usual.

"The well's dried up!" they heard Grandma shouting from the bottom of the hill. "There's not a drop of water."

Uncle kept drinking his beer; he wasn't too worried. He was already wishing he'd stayed home, camped out in front of the television.

"There's no water? My god, there are worse things," he said to the children.

Every summer Uncle would tell them, "At the base of the hill, near the well, there's treasure buried, huge pots of gold. When the aliens come to abduct me, I'm going to dig them up and bring them to Mars."

"Don't forget the beer," Grandma would quip, but Uncle would pay her no mind.

"Why don't we dig them up right now?" the children would ask, curious.

"Because it's not the right time," Uncle would say.

The children believed him because back home he had a sizable collection of *Arka*, a magazine dedicated to all things supernatural—UFOs, witches, mermaids, ghosts—which the children would regularly read. From time to time, the children would also find porn he'd hidden in album sleeves. They couldn't understand why he put them there, why he hid them.

"Grandma, Grandma, where did this come from?" the grandchildren had asked one time.

Grandma, who would come over to tidy up Uncle's apartment, had supplied a quick answer.

"Your grandpa found those in the hallway a while back, and brought them over for cleaning the windows."

The children were naive, but they weren't stupid. Obviously Grandma was hiding something.

Soon after that, the next time they went to Uncle's place, the dirty magazines were no longer among the records, but the issues of *Arka* remained in their usual place. To the children, nothing made sense; the pictures they saw in *Arka* were stranger than the ones in the magazines Uncle allegedly used to clean the windows, but nevertheless, they hadn't been removed.

Grandma slowly began making her way back uphill to the cottage. Uncle watched her with a smile.

"How will you take a bath in a barrel if there's no water?" the children asked him.

"I'll bring the barrel home," Uncle replied, and kept drinking.

"We need to call on Zoran," Grandma said. "This well is done for."

"Why not take the kids to see him?" Uncle asked as he finished his beer and opened up another. "The car can't make it up such a steep slope. You can all go for a walk in the woods."

Grandma looked at him but didn't say anything. She turned to the grandchildren and asked, "Want to go for a walk with me?"

"We'd rather go with Uncle," they replied.

Grandma kissed their foreheads, fixed her gaze on her son again, and said calmly, "Tell Zoran to hurry. This is already the third well that's dried up. Your sister doesn't have any water, either."

Uncle rose reluctantly from the bench and put on the T-shirt he'd taken off only minutes before due to the July heat.

"Maybe the car could make it to Zoran's house. The climb isn't all that steep," he said.

3.

The children bounced around in the backseat. It was sweltering, and their bare legs stuck to the vinyl upholstery. This was before the internet, so they couldn't complain to their friends about how hot and miserable it was. Uncle grumbled to himself. He was a bachelor, and Grandma was trying to get him to drive her to the country every weekend. He hated going to Smoluća, and he hated his mother.

"We could still go swimming in the creek," said one of the grandchildren.

"We could," said Uncle. "We could, but we won't."

They stopped halfway up the hill, when Uncle could barely inch the car any further. The children loved to ride with the parking brake up; it was fun to watch Uncle struggle to get the car to the top. They finally arrived at Zoran's house to find hens and geese darting around out front. A dog was chained up and barking furiously.

"Stay in the car," said Uncle. "I'll be quick."

Zoran's house had a dirt floor. The hens were free to wander inside. Two mangy, lethargic cats sprawled by the front door. Uncle had to step over them. At the table, with a bottle of beer, sat Zoran. He stared absently out a small window.

"Hi there, Zoran," said Uncle.

"Hey," replied Zoran. "What brings you here?"

"Our well's dried up."

"Figures, there's a big drought."

"We need to drill a new one, someplace where there's no problem with the water. Though it's all the same to me. With or without water, I'm cursed with a bitchy old lady."

"Don't talk that way about your mother," said Zoran.

He didn't sound convincing.

"The old broad gets on everyone's nerves. She drives my sister nuts too. All she does is pop pills, hoard trash, and nag us. She's been unbearable since Dad died."

Zoran fixed Uncle with a questioning look.

"Sometimes it's a blessing to lose a parent," he said.

Uncle seemed not to hear him. He studied his beer bottle.

"You want another?" asked the well digger.

"Sure."

Zoran turned to the refrigerator behind him.

"You have a lot of work these days?" asked Uncle.

"Yeah, but I can take a look at the problem tomorrow."

"Great," said Uncle, gulping his beer for the hundredth time.

Meanwhile, the children, of course, hadn't listened to their uncle, and leaped from the car. The geese were angry, and one chased them around the yard. The girls bounded, out of breath, into Zoran's doorway. The cats ran for cover. The dog wouldn't stop barking.

"These are your beautiful nieces?" Zoran asked Uncle.

"Yes, our three treasures," replied Uncle. "And my eldest sister has two sons and a daughter. They're just wonderful," he added.

The girls looked at Zoran. It seemed to them they'd seen his face somewhere. But they couldn't stand his laugh. It evoked, one of the girls would recall later, a forest monster they'd read about in an issue of *Arka*. The monster who'd drag you to the depths of the icy lake when you sat staring at your reflection. Before, they hadn't known the monster's name, but when they set their eyes on the well digger, it dawned on them. The monster was called Zoran and had emerged from the forest. He no longer needed the lake.

4.

"Eight hundred marks minimum?" Grandma said when they got back.

"That's what Zoran said," Uncle replied. "He said it's not worth digging down less than eight meters, and considering that a lot of the wells around here have dried up, he'd definitely need to go twice as deep."

"It strikes me as odd that he has so much work, but lives so poorly. What does he spend all that money on?"

Uncle said nothing. He wiped his forehead with his hand—he was soaked in sweat.

The children went over to their aunt's house and sat on the stairs. They were waiting for their cousins to arrive and their aunt to bring cake. Grandma had to watch her sugar and no longer baked cakes or pies, to the great dismay of her grandchildren. The girls flung stones at the dusty road.

"What do you think Uncle's treasure is like?" asked one of them.

"Big!" replied the youngest one.

She indicated the exact size with her hands.

"From here to the moon!" she added.

"It must be full of gold," the eldest one concluded, continuing to daydream.

Just as the girls got up to walk along the gravel path, their cousins arrived. They feasted on lunch. The adults discussed the drought and the new wells. Grandma and Auntie eventually decided to drill just one and share the expense.

"I only hope," said Grandma, "that Zoran finds water. Sometimes it seems like the whole area's dried up. Like the water fled somewhere."

"It must've fled to a place with better people," said Uncle, looking up at the sky.

The next day Zoran came to investigate what was happening with the water. He carried two wires for welding, bent on one end. He grasped them like improvised handles and began tromping around near Grandma's old well. The wires reacted weakly: they didn't fan out. The water line was elsewhere.

Zoran kept searching for water. The children watched him. They agreed he was weird and they didn't like him—he looked like a big fake. When they couldn't stand watching him anymore, they left for the shed. They perched on a woodpile and discussed whether it was possible to identify and expose a monster.

"Maybe his face would change if we took away those wires?" said one boy.

"I don't think that would make any difference," said one of the girls. "Yesterday he didn't have them, and he looked the same."

While the children deliberated, the adults followed the well digger's progress anxiously.

"Okay, let's drill here," said Zoran after some time.

Everyone gave a collective sigh of relief; only the children still watched with concern.

"What if instead of water he finds the treasure?" they wondered.

5.

Zoran said that after he'd dug the new well, he'd fill in the old one. The children didn't want to be bothered with the drilling, even though, of course, they recognized its amusing sexual connotations. They knew the well digger had a special van with a drill attachment, that he would install concrete pipes, a pump. They'd overheard the adults talking about it.

While he was preparing the drill, Zoran spoke with the other adults about politics (the nineties were beginning) and inflation (the dinar had never been so weak), but mostly about the disappearance of some old women from the neighboring village.

"Not one of them suffered from dementia," said Grandma in a distraught voice. "It's odd that the women would vanish just like that."

"They were alone," Uncle said. "Their children didn't take care of them. Maybe they took them abroad."

"Or to a nursing home," added Auntie.

"It's strange," Zoran said. "Sometimes I get scared living alone."

"You're young, nothing will happen to you," Grandma reassured him.

Auntie laughed. "Maybe they took the water with them."

"Anything's possible," said Uncle.

But he was wrong. Not all things were possible. For example, it wasn't possible for the children to ever like Zoran. They watched him carefully from a great distance.

"We should follow him," the eldest granddaughter proposed.

The rest of the children disagreed.

"He lives too far away. Let's go to the field and eat roasted corn instead."

In the evening, the children gathered around the fire, laughing and playing. They had stopped thinking about Zoran, and were no longer watching him.

Later that night, Zoran dragged two enormous bags into their yard. Cement? Construction scrap? No one could see him; everyone was sleeping. The children were arranged like an orderly row of magazines, from the first issue to the last. Uncle had fallen asleep on the couch. Grandma lay in her bed. And the neighboring cottage sat in darkness. You couldn't even see your hand right in front of your face. The dog wasn't barking at Zoran's slog through the yard; there wasn't a dog because no one lived there anymore. Who would take care of feeding a dog? The children wanted one, but children want everything.

Zoran, under cover of the Smoluća night, continued tending to the wells he planned to fill in the next day. He threw one of the bags into each of the dried-up wells. Actually, he didn't throw them—he lowered them slowly, using a rope. Before he began, his pulling accidentally caused one of the bags to tear, but no one could see what lay inside. He was quiet, shoveling a thin layer of earth over both of the bags, covering them quickly, then heading back home. He didn't stumble once; he knew every stone, every slope. He'd grown up there and knew the area better than all the other residents combined.

While he slowly climbed the hill, his mind was

somewhere else. He wasn't thinking about his child-hood. He wasn't thinking about his family, his mother, his father, who'd spent the whole day in the fields. Who'd left him in a barrel, or tied him to a tree, so there'd be no worrying about where he was or what he was getting into while unsupervised. He'd spent those years looking up from the bottom, circling a small tree on a short leash. But had he really grown up? Had he ever managed to break out of the barrel, to untie the knot and get away from the tree? Had he freed himself from his horrible parents, their neglect? He never asked himself these things.

He walked slowly; the climb was nothing to him. In the morning, he carried on his work from the previous night without incident, but he couldn't do it for long. He was exhausted, it was plain to see.

"I'm going home," he said hastily.

It wasn't even noon. Grandma patted him on the shoulder.

"You don't look well, Zoran," she said. "Why don't you lie down here? You need to eat something."

Zoran tried to leave, but he couldn't. Grandma was stubborn, and even Uncle began to insist.

"Mom's right," he said. "Go lie down."

"Okay," said Zoran. "Okay, I'll just stretch out for a bit."

The children were horrified. They didn't want him lying in their bed.

While Zoran slept, the grandchildren decided to go to the old wells and check on their enemy's work.

They were nervous on the way, trudging through the grass, trudging and trudging until finally, one of the girls saw something shiny.

"Look!" she said.

An antique gold ring gleamed in the eldest grand-daughter's palm. The children gathered around it. They gaped at the piece of jewelry, utterly amazed.

"The treasure really exists!" exclaimed the youngest.

"Then surely Martians do too," concluded her cousin.

Zoran slept nearby, one of his eyes still open, his ears pricked up. The monster had emerged from the forest and given the children a gift. The summer slowly came to a happy close.

THE TALUS OF MADAME LIKEN

Lichen: nature's chaos. A body of algae and mushroom, the symbiosis blanketing the corpse found in the nearby forest. The police ruled it a violent death. Someone had covered the naked male body with lichen, all but the lips, gently parted.

My house was in the immediate vicinity; I watched the coroner, the police vehicles, through the window. Who would identify the deceased? No papers were found on him. No traces. I smiled—all these years, and this was the first body they'd discovered.

"Mrs. Liken!" a young policeman called through the open window.

"Just a moment!"

"Could we ask you a few questions for our report?"

"Of course. I'll do anything to help."

All clichés. The medicine bottles worked in my favor. They were my alibi. I was sleeping. I didn't hear a thing.

"I was sleeping. I didn't hear a thing."

"Thank you. Let us know if you notice anything."

"I will, of course! Goodbye."

I noticed that you don't have a clue. Should I tell them that? But ignorance isn't suspicious. It would be strange were it otherwise.

When the young policeman returned, I kept calm. He didn't even know how to pronounce my last name, and I didn't correct him. To appear even more convincing, I asked whether I was in any danger, whether I was safe.

"Don't worry, Mrs. Leeken, we have everything under control."

I acted as though a weight had been lifted from my heart.

"That's a relief," I said.

It rained for days and the yard was unbearably muddy. Everything outside got drenched and morphed into an uglier version of itself.

The policeman kept coming by, grasping for every little crumb, genuinely worried because the investigation hadn't yielded anything. He asked me to describe my neighbors.

"You see how far away our houses are from one another."

"Sure, I understand," said the policeman, "but still—the town has a general store, a bar and restaurant, a gas station . . . Surely you know some of your neighbors."

"We've met," I replied, "but it's not polite to inquire about the details of other people's lives."

As soon as the errand boy left, I plopped down on the sofa. There was some reality TV show on about a famous American family. I enjoyed sticking my nose in other people's business, watching them get tortured by the shit they'd been dealt. You could learn a lot from the fools on TV, just as you could from everyday life.

Right as I was about to change the channel, someone knocked on my door. I thought the policeman had returned. I cracked the door open just enough to peek out and kindly say that I was busy. A young woman stood on the porch, sopping wet. She asked if she could come in. She seemed exhausted.

She had addressed me as "neighbor," but I'd never seen her before.

"Where did you come from?" I asked once she was inside.

"From the north," she said curtly.

She was shivering. I gave her a clean towel and clothes to change into. She took them without a word; she didn't even thank me. I returned to the sofa. I heard the young woman undressing in the bathroom. If I had to describe her succinctly, I'd say she was very beautiful. Later I'd reflect on her appearance, but at that moment it didn't mean much to me.

"You said from the north, but where exactly?" I asked when she reappeared.

"The mountains," she replied. "I live in a cottage near the lake."

"Did your car break down?"

"I don't have a car. I go everywhere on foot."

"It's not the season for walking," I said. "It's cold, and people are idiots."

She nodded. "They are."

A kindred spirit, or a victim? I couldn't immediately tell. I stared at her curiously, unable to control myself. Her hair was gathered into a bun. She'd thrown on my sweater, which was too big for her. Then, completely by accident, I noticed her feet.

"Do you come to town often?"

"I wouldn't call this place a town," she said.

I wasn't thrown off.

"Do you come down from the mountain often?"

"No."

I asked how she made a living, whether she had anyone to keep her company.

"I have hunting dogs. I'm not alone."

I made tea for both of us. The young woman drank hers slowly, like she was in no hurry to leave, but as soon as the rain let up, she collected her clothes, slipped on her boots, and made her way to the door. She thanked me for the sweater, said she'd return it as soon as she could. She waved and then disappeared into the mist. I was excited. I'd forgotten to ask the young woman her name.

When they found the next body in the woods, it wasn't mine. I asked around to find out who the victim was—a local man who'd had a bad reputation for illegal hunting. He hadn't deserved to die, though. The news hit me hard; we'd been good friends. I knew that he'd been struggling with financial problems.

Maybe he'd owed the wrong people money and couldn't pay?

The days passed slowly. The weather worsened—winter was finally arriving. No one could get to the lake; the road was pure mud. I didn't leave the house. I'd call the store with a list of supplies to be delivered. Everyone in town knew one another, of course. We were like family, but the police didn't need to know that. The death of our neighbor had shaken us. Some more, some less, but no one was unaffected.

I spent most of my days devising a plan for when the young woman returned. I wasted a lot of time thinking about her. I watched TV, lying down, waiting for something interesting to happen, something that would spur me to act. I'd never hurt my neighbors, but strangers meant nothing to me. The young woman meant nothing to me.

A powerful storm is the most thrilling weather. I watched it through the window: the thrashing trees, things flying through the air that weren't meant to leave the ground. The colors were impressive. Everything outside matched my mood. I was standing as usual at the window, listening to the thunder, when I noticed the young woman approaching. I couldn't see which direction she'd come from. I opened the door as soon as I heard her steps on the porch.

"You always come at an infelicitous moment," I said.

She didn't know what "infelicitous" meant.

"What are you doing here?" I asked.

"I came to return your sweater."

"Now? In such terrible weather?"

"The weather is ideal."

She wasn't wet at all. It was like the storm had skipped over her completely: there wasn't a drop of water on her raincoat.

"Your sweater," she said.

She pushed it under my nose.

"There really wasn't any rush."

"I don't like debts."

"Would you like something to drink?" I asked.

"Sure."

The young woman wore her muddy boots through the entryway and into the living room, but she didn't care. She flung herself into an armchair and allowed me to watch her for some time in silence. My excitement grew palpable. The last time I'd been this excited was while beating that young man to death, the one who'd been found in the woods not long before. While I was killing him, I had to wipe my mouth with my sleeve every now and then because I couldn't stop salivating.

I briefly escaped to the kitchen to calm down. I forgot to make the tea. I was still clutching the sweater.

"Aren't you afraid of being out in this weather?" I asked the young woman. "The thunder is terrible."

"I'm not afraid of thunder," she said.

"Not one bit?"

"Not one bit."

She acted so confidently, as if nothing could hurt her, as if nothing scared her. Not even me, though my appearance didn't exactly inspire trust.

"Did you know the man who was murdered?" she asked suddenly.

Her tone surprised me. It was accusing.

"Which one? They found two."

"The first one."

"I didn't. He wasn't from around here."

I was overtaken by suspicion. Maybe she worked for the police. She seemed intelligent. She would understand what the young policeman couldn't.

"It was shocking that they found the body so close to my house," I said calmly.

"It must've given you the creeps," she said. "Who wouldn't it."

The creeps? I didn't know what the creeps felt like. I'd never felt them.

"It did," I said. "It was awful."

While saying this, I felt a hole in my sweater. It was big enough to fit my index finger through. It seemed to have been made by a bullet.

"Your friend," the woman said, smiling, "was wearing that sweater when he died."

I looked at her in disbelief.

"I have no friends," I said.

"True," she said, "not anymore."

We stared at each other across the table, where the young woman had propped her muddy boots. She was letting me know that she was now the master

41

and I the apprentice, one who still had much to learn about the art of violence and suffering. My head began to hurt. I felt a pressure in my temples, as if the young woman had taken my head in her hands and begun to squeeze.

"I don't plan on staying long," she said, not budging.

"All right."

I contemplated my next move. There was a model airplane close at hand; I could bash her head in with it. But I quickly dismissed the idea. The young woman looked toy-proof.

"Do you often go hunting?" I asked to distract myself from my headache.

Instead of answering, she reached into the backpack she'd brought with her and retrieved a thin notebook.

"I like to cross a debt off my list once I've settled it," she said.

Her drawing of the line across the paper lasted an eternity.

"You mean the sweater?" I asked.

She didn't answer. She returned the notebook to her backpack and finally stood up.

"It's time for me to go home."

"Yes," I replied absently.

She paused for a moment at the door.

"That young man was important to me."

No more would she call me "neighbor." We'd returned to being strangers.

We didn't shake hands at the door; she didn't even acknowledge me. While she was walking away, I saw—or it seemed to me I saw—that the young woman's muddy boots had been replaced with gold sandals. At the very edge of the property, near the road, before she was lost to the landscape, her silhouette no longer had a backpack thrown over its shoulders. On an unfamiliar back hung a bow and arrow. I recalled the naked man's body, his lips—gently parted. I wanted them to breathe in the air once more. I shivered, I'd like to say because of the cold. But my reality had completely changed. I could no longer lie so calmly.

ABBY

"I don't want to eat that," I said, pushing away the plate. I didn't even know what it was that I didn't want, but it stank. As if someone had served me something rotten.

"I'm sorry, I didn't know you no longer liked shellfish."

Only then did I look: I'd pushed away a plate of mussels. My mouth began to water.

"I'll take a little then."

It was strange to suddenly notice things. At times I'd been feeling like I was falling asleep. I knew there was a disorder where people would fall asleep out of nowhere—narcolepsy—but I could tell that wasn't what was happening to me. After taking a bite, I noticed a cut and a bruise on my right forearm: I'd fought with something, against someone. I peered at the wound.

"Does it hurt?"

"Not really. When did I get this?"

"Recently."

Nothing was clear to me. The only thing I

45

remembered was that a couple days before, I'd called the speaking clock. I'd dialed 95, and instead of the usual voice telling me the time, I'd heard a woman's voice declaring, "*Ai difensori della libertà*: you were a slave then, and you're a slave now."

I'd written these words down on a slip of paper as if I'd expected to hear them instead of the time. I'd been puzzled, but obviously not too much. Over the mussels, I remembered that a few years back, I'd day-dreamed often about becoming a different person. I'd longed for something to stick my finger in, like a socket—it would carry the shock of electricity—and I'd proceed through life transformed. Better, natu-rally. I reflected as well on the fact that, even though I lacked any qualities that would warrant a strong sense of self, I possessed a superiority complex all the same: like I knew everything and could only continue to improve. The man I was dining with noticed my mind was elsewhere.

"Is everything all right?"

I didn't know what to say.

"Of course!"

It turned out I was an excellent liar. I felt like someone had thrown me into a scene, as I didn't rec-ognize the man I was eating with. I recalled things that had nothing to do with him. Maybe I was sup-posed to be scared?

"Are you remembering something?" the man asked.

"Excuse me?"

"Don't worry, the doctor said your memory will return little by little."

I had no idea what he was talking about. I speculated.

"I lose my memory every five minutes?"

"It's like you're resetting. The doctor said it'll take at least a year for your memory to be completely restored."

Parts of it were irrevocably lost, I told myself. How could I possibly collect all the pieces that made me a good liar who loved mussels?

"I bought you a diary for moments like these. As soon as you remember something, you can write it down."

He thrust a little black notebook into my hand. I took it and flipped through it. There were all kinds of notes inside, from the most basic things like my favorite color or food—it seemed these changed constantly—to illegible scribbling. The memory of the strange phone call was underlined in red marker. It appeared to be something important.

"What sort of call was this?" I asked.

"I don't know," he said. "We agreed that I wouldn't look at your notes to respect your privacy."

"Who are you exactly?"

The man's face twitched. He hadn't taken my question well.

"Abby, it's me, John. Your husband."

My name, therefore, was Abby. I assumed my husband really was my husband, even though I had no evidence. And then I noticed something odd—we weren't speaking English.

"How is it possible that our names are Abby and John when we don't speak English?"

As soon as I said this, John, my husband, grabbed me by the shoulders and started to shake me, as if trying to hear whether something inside me had spoiled, or broken. He returned to the beginning, starting our dialogue from before:

"I'm sorry, I didn't know you no longer liked shellfish."

I pretended I didn't know we were repeating the conversation.

"I'll take a little then."

When we arrived at the moment when I had mentioned that we weren't speaking English, I went silent. I remembered that I'd learned Swahili, that I spoke French and German fluently. Was I a spy? I also knew Russian, Arabic, and Spanish. It was obvious that languages came easily to me. Who is this man? I kept asking myself. Who is Abby?

"I should make a phone call," I said abruptly.

"Why?" the man asked.

Someone rang a neighbor's doorbell. I flinched.

"It could help me remember a number. Maybe using the phone will help."

"You're right."

Turning my back to John, I dialed the speaking clock.

"The current time is exactly 21 hours, 4 minutes, and 295 seconds."

295 seconds? Last time I'd checked, a minute was much shorter. Maybe this was some kind of sign. I dialed 95 again.

"The current time is exactly 21 hours, 5 minutes, and 15 seconds."

"Did you remember anything?" John asked.

"Unfortunately not. I'd like to be alone for a little while."

"I understand," he said. "I'll be in the living room. Whenever you're ready, come join me."

I stood there for a few minutes. John, if that really was his name, sat in the adjacent room, in front of the television. I gazed at myself in the mirror above the phone—I looked well, but I hardly felt that way. I jotted down "295" in my notes and went to sit next to my husband. He observed me with interest. Did he want me to say something?

"Do you want me to say something?"

"No, no. Just sit. I don't want to rush you."

"I don't understand how I lost my memory. What happened?"

"You were hit by a car," John said.

Surely I hadn't been in an accident. There wasn't a scratch on the rest of my body; only my arm hurt. He'd looked me straight in the eye and lied to me. I felt as though it wasn't the first time. I'd been in deep shit all along. This, at least, was clear.

"What was the car like?"

"What do you mean, what was the car like?"

"What type of car was it?"

"A limousine."

He was good; he didn't even blink. Psychopath.

"Were you the one driving?"

"God forbid!"

Saying I wanted to go to bed, I left to lie down. He followed me. He was well-built, good-looking; we fucked, but I felt nothing. I'd never loved this man. I fell asleep thinking about it. I hoped everything would make sense in the morning, but it didn't. I woke up late, with a headache. My arm had stopped hurting.

He made mussels for lunch again. I pretended I didn't know I'd had them the day before. I pushed the plate away and we started from the beginning:

"I don't want to eat that."

"I'm sorry, I didn't know you no longer liked shellfish."

"I'll take a little then."

While I was eating, I watched him. I assumed he was there to monitor me. I couldn't remember why I was dangerous.

"How long have I been home?"

"Two weeks."

"Two weeks already? I don't remember a thing."

I knew he'd been reading my diary, because he wouldn't let me make a phone call.

"You'll upset yourself," he said. "You won't remember anything."

I didn't give up so easily.

"Why don't you go in the living room?" I said. "I'll clean up."

John left, and I collected the dishes. I tapped the edge of a plate with a fork to make it sound like I was carrying them into the kitchen. Then I dialed the speaking clock. The voice announced, "The current time is exactly 14 hours, 11 minutes, and 005 seconds."

I knew I couldn't write down any more numbers because John would see. Yesterday, 295; today, 005. Tomorrow? I went to bed annoyed. John didn't disturb me, but I sensed he wanted to. I turned my back to him and pretended to be asleep.

The next day was December 6, and he said we were going to celebrate his birthday. But we spent the whole day just like any other. The date was most likely important for some other reason. Though, admittedly, a birthday was no small matter. I couldn't even remember when mine was, after all. While John was in the other room, I persisted in making my phone call. I dialed the speaking clock, but didn't hear anything unusual. I dialed 295005 to see if it had any significance.

"Hello?" I heard from the other end.

"Hello?" I said.

"Hey, it's you! You're back!"

I hung up. The woman obviously hadn't known what she was talking about. Back from where? Had I gone somewhere?

Mildly unnerved by the unfamiliar woman's voice,

I picked up my diary and just then noticed how strange my handwriting was. The words sometimes looked like they'd been scrawled by a child. They'd been written by an unsure hand, as if the hand was just learning how to write.

I showered reluctantly and nearly slipped in the bathtub. Everything felt difficult. When I saw that I would indeed fall if I wasn't careful, I crouched under the spout, getting my head wet. I began to wash myself, and when I got to my feet I felt bumps under my toes, like they'd been made by tiny, tingling needles. I wasn't a drug addict, so it had to be something else. I couldn't ask John; I needed to call that woman. The thought that I could call only her kept me up all night. I watched John, unable to recognize him.

In the morning, while John was still sleeping, I called 295005.

"Do you remember?" asked the woman's voice.

"Unfortunately not," I replied sheepishly. "Who am I speaking to?"

"Are you okay?"

"What is my name?" I asked.

"Excuse me?"

"What is my name?" I repeated.

At that moment, John entered the room.

"What are you doing? Who are you talking to?" he asked.

"Wrong number," I lied. "The ringing woke me."

"No one's ever called this number."

"Some woman wanted to talk to her son. I told her she misdialed."

"Where was she calling from? Did she tell you?" John was visibly nervous.

"No," I said.

"Okay. Let's have breakfast."

I couldn't even manage a bite. John regarded me strangely.

"Are you sure that's all the woman said?" he asked.

"What woman?"

"Forget it," he said, continuing to eat.

After some time, John said he needed to go to the store. I nodded, not listening to his reason. I looked at the clock.

I didn't know what I was supposed to do while he was gone. Masturbate? Escape? I wasn't sure what I should be prioritizing. I went to John's study and tried to open the locked drawers of his desk. I searched everywhere for the key: under the bed, in the dresser, in the kitchen. I accidentally discovered a safe behind a painting. I didn't know the combination. I made a few attempts, but nothing worked. While I was setting the painting back in place, I heard John entering the apartment.

"That was fast," I said.

"I promised I wouldn't be long."

"When can I go to the store?" I asked.

"When the doctor says you can," he replied.

While John explained that it would be easy for

me to get lost in the street because I didn't know who I was, he unpacked the groceries. An apple fell to the floor, and when he bent down to pick it up, a chain with a small key slipped out from under his collar. I immediately thought of the desk drawers.

"I like your necklace," I said. "Can I have it?"

John eyed me suspiciously.

"Why?"

"I like it. Is it a gift from me?"

"No."

He placed the chain back underneath his shirt.

"It was a gift from my parents," he added.

"Do I like jewelry?" I asked.

John didn't respond. He disappeared into the other room. I waited impatiently for night to fall so I could get ahold of the necklace. It was all I thought about the entire day.

When John finally fell asleep that night, I slowly removed his necklace. I went to his desk and unlocked both drawers. I planned to inspect them the next day.

I didn't want to ask John too many questions about myself, lest he suspect something. I kept pretending to be lost, like I was perpetually forgetting where I was and what I was doing. John prepared mussels again and pushed them under my nose. I didn't know why he did that.

"I need to go to the store," he said while we were sitting at the table. "I won't be long."

I calculated that I had less than ten minutes. The store was clearly nearby. As soon as John closed the door behind him, I went to the study. He hadn't checked the drawers; they were still unlocked. In the first one I found utility bills, empty envelopes. In the second, there were documents I didn't examine carefully, along with a charger—for a cell phone or other device, I assumed.

"Shit!" I said, glancing at the clock.

Just then I heard John unlocking the door.

"Shit!" I repeated.

"You don't look well," John said when he laid eyes on me. "Is everything all right?"

"I'm all right, everything's all right," I lied.

I was livid. I wanted to kill John. I didn't know what was stopping me.

In the meantime, John locked both drawers. He disconnected the phone, saying the bills were too high. My nervousness grew to the point that I felt I'd explode if something didn't change.

John always went out for ten minutes, never longer. While he was away, I tried to open the safe. I used his birthday and the numbers I'd heard over the phone, but nothing worked. I asked him to buy me bobby pins—I wanted to pick the locks on his drawers—but he refused. He said he preferred my hair loose.

"It's more feminine," he said.

It seemed we spent the whole day at the dining room table, in the kitchen, or in front of the television. John had a routine we were both obligated to follow.

"Mussels again?" I cried.

"What's wrong with mussels?" he asked.

"Nothing. I'll take a little."

I didn't want to risk it, so I laid off the drawers for a few nights. It always felt awkward to touch John's neck and unbutton his pajamas to get to the key. But then I couldn't stand it anymore: I slipped off the necklace again and opened the drawers. I didn't wait for my ten minutes but immediately spread the contents of the second drawer on the carpet. As if shuffling a pack of cards, I sifted through the papers and randomly pulled a few of them out. I returned the rest, locked the drawers, and went back to bed. I hid the documents in my pillowcase. In the morning, I went to the bathroom and studied them for a long time.

First I read an agreement between John and a bank. He'd taken out a huge loan the year before. It didn't say for what. Another document had a watermark, but nothing was written on it. The others were also blank.

No luck, I thought.

"Are you finished?" John asked.

He rattled the doorknob.

"Just a minute," I said.

"Hurry up."

I shoved the papers into my pants and went out.

At breakfast we chatted about food, and I took the opportunity to mention money. I said that perhaps I should get a job.

"We don't have money for the phone, isn't that sad?"

"You can't work, that's not right," he said.

"Why?" I asked.

"You need to get well first."

It seemed to him I'd never be well; I'd never be able to work or go outside. Watching him over the meal, my thoughts returned to violence. The problem was I didn't really know who or where I was. I couldn't harm him until I found out.

He's lying about us not having money, I thought. We eat like kings.

And truly, the refrigerator was full of delicacies. John was constantly devouring enormous amounts of food. Compared to his, my appetite was negligible. I ate only the mussels he gave me. Here and there I sampled something sweet, but food gave me no pleasure. I ate only because John ate.

"How do you stay in shape when you eat so much?" I asked him.

"I exercise regularly."

I'd never seen him exercise. He didn't work on his abs; he didn't go to the gym. It was impossible that in the ten minutes he was gone from the apartment he went shopping and lifted weights too. I watched how voraciously he consumed all the food on the table and drank tea as if his life depended on it. I wanted to tell him to stop being such a pig, but I didn't want to hear his reply. I didn't want to hear his voice.

It was time to watch TV, then time to eat again. After dinner, more TV, and finally bed. In the middle of the night, John began to talk in his sleep. What I heard was helpful.

It was mostly nonsense, but periodically he uttered the combination to his safe, like he was making an effort not to forget it. He repeated it so many times that I memorized it with ease. I didn't hurry to the safe right away; I needed daylight. John soon began to snore. I fell asleep after counting about three hundred sheep.

The combination was very simple, almost stupidly so. After breakfast, during his ten minutes, I succeeded in opening the safe and exploring its contents. There was no money or weapons—just one USB stick, a sheet of paper, and a photo of me. I turned it over to see what was on the back. There I read: *Serial number: 295-005, Model: Abby*. I stared in disbelief. On the paper were printed instructions. I realized the charger I'd seen in the drawer wasn't for a phone, but for me. I took the USB, shoved it in my pocket, and closed the safe. John entered the apartment, elated.

"I just paid the last loan installment," he said.

I hit him on the head, hard. He fell to his knees.

While he was moaning in pain, I ran out the open door. I remembered that *Ai difensori della libertà* was in San Marino. I set off for there.

Walking quickly, I noticed a few drops of John's blood on my boots. I bent down, and saw my reflection in their shine.

295005 is an excellent name, I thought, wiping off the blood. It's sonorous and easy to remember.

I tossed the USB on the ground and stomped on it. I resolved that no one would stick anything into me anymore.

ASJA 5.0

The future is impossible to predict because there isn't just one future. I used to consider this a stupid claim, but really, I think—sitting with neat rows of pills arranged in front of me, pills I've diligently collected over the past months—the future is fragmentary: in one future I'll take a pill, in another I won't, and in the third, fifth, tenth, I may not even be in a position to choose.

While I'm counting the pills, I get a message from Asja: "Be patient a little longer."

"I don't trust you," I reply.

My fingers are so numb I can hardly text. I can't trust her. She, too, is Asja, and they're closing in on her too—her life likewise hangs by a thread.

I bar the front door with the wardrobe and sofa. I fear one of us is patiently lying in wait, maybe this very one who's sending me messages. Who knows, maybe they need to destroy me if they want to stay alive themselves. Maybe I'm the only one who'd rather hurt myself than someone else. The others clearly don't have such qualms. There are no rows of pills arranged in front of them, but knives, hand grenades—anything capable of wiping out the competition, anything that can make the future go their way.

I don't go near the window, even though I've lowered the blinds and closed the heavy velvet curtains. It's impossible to see me, but I'm still expecting them to retaliate. I don't know which of them Kreanga might send. Best be on the lookout.

"I'm deleting you," reads the message.

"How can I verify that?" I ask.

"Try looking up your ID number."

I check the internet: I don't exist. She's even deleted my blog.

"Thank you," I reply.

I don't know enough about computers; I'm not sure if Asja is lying to me. I place the pills back in their tin box. Only one of them is toxic, but I have no way of knowing which because they're all the same color.

"I've let the others know we should meet outside the abandoned pharmaceutical plant," writes Asja.

"All right."

"Be there at midnight," she says.

"Okay."

I have no intention of going. I search for a hunting knife in the wardrobe blocking the door. I know I have a few, but I can't find them anywhere.

I should've been more organized, I tell myself.

Eventually I find an old knife with a carved

rosewood hilt. As soon as I touch it, I know that Kreanga is thinking of me. When things were still okay between us, we would go to the forest to hunt together. Somewhere along the way, Kreanga would shove his hand down my pants.

"The forest is yours," I'd say, "but what you've grabbed—that is not."

He laughed then, but later it became clear to him that I really meant it.

When I arrived at his castle in '93, during one of the worst famines in recent memory, I'd been soaked in sweat. But Kreanga hadn't sent me to the bathroom so I could wash myself, as I'd naively expected. Instead he ushered me into his bedroom so he could, as he said, "lick you from head to toe." It's hard to believe what those who weren't hungry in those days gave themselves license to do.

"No thank you," I said. "I need lodging—tomorrow I'll be on my way."

"Where are you headed?" he asked.

He smiled. I could already tell there was no room for novelty in his appetites: Kreanga loved what his father loved, what his grandfather and great-grandfather had loved, and I was there just to confirm his proclivities, to reinforce his fetish. I proposed that I pay for the room by writing porn for him. He agreed to it faster than I'd anticipated.

"Why aren't you here?" reads Asja's message. "It's midnight."

I flinch, interrupting the memory.

"I haven't managed to get there yet," I lie, clenching the knife between my teeth so it's easier to text.

"You're not the only one who's worried, we all are," she replies.

Her anger is obvious even without the use of emojis. My thoughts are straining, like frayed rope—everything hangs from a thread: all the Asjas, Kreanga, everything I did well and poorly, and, maybe worst of all, my blood. If I hadn't let Kreanga take a sample of it, I wouldn't be here now. I wouldn't have a knife between my teeth; I wouldn't be feverishly sending these stupid, deceitful messages.

"Tomorrow, same time, same place. If you're not there, we're coming for you," writes Asja.

I'm not scared, but I can't fall asleep. I turn off all the lights, slump in an armchair, pull a blanket up to my chin. The knife sits in my lap. When I close my eyes, I return to my daydream: I see Kreanga moving his lips as he read what I'd written him that week. Utterly obsessed, he declared himself delighted. I tried to explain that few people had time for nostalgia anymore, but he ignored my remark.

"People are dying of hunger," I continued.

"This is excellent!"

Kreanga never listened to me. He waved his arms around excitedly as if he'd never read anything in his whole life. I'm not the best writer, I know that, but Kreanga, having never read D. Elmiger, had no idea what good literature looked like.

The moon overhead is incredibly close now,

enormous, like a nipple wanting to breastfeed my paranoia.

"Everything's going to be okay," I tell myself. "Everything's going to be okay."

But the blanket feels too heavy; it's like Kreanga is sitting on my chest. I'm sweating profusely. I look over at my bookcase: the collected works of D. Elmiger, slim volumes full of lascivious scenes and descriptions that we all devoured in disbelief. Had people really done such things? Had they really?

In the morning, I count the pills again, convinced that only this will help me sort out my problems. My sweat hangs heavy in the air. The smell doesn't bother me; my brain perceives it as something distinctly literary, like a motif I often used for Kreanga—the fetid sweat of a woman's shaved armpit. Every sex scene, every sentence, needed to be saturated with pungent odors, liters and liters of saliva and mucus; otherwise, Kreanga would show his disapproval by tossing the draft in the trash.

One day we sat beneath a tree, plum maybe, and he read a story of mine that I'd set right there in his garden.

"The best you've written so far!" he said. "I love when it's two women."

I always carried the book by D. Elmiger with me and copied her descriptions whenever I ran out of inspiration. I pretended to understand what I was writing, as if I'd actually experienced sex and was now sharing the knowledge with my titillated reader.

Instead of a day or two, I stayed at Kreanga's castle for three years. When I finally left, I fled with one bundle on my back. The knife in my lap I'd found in his pantry, along with some cured meat and the scent that's never left my nose: the scent of prosperity.

Kreanga's hope was to be the first man to achieve an erection in god knows how many years, and it drove him to behave like it could happen at any moment. He used different methods: toys, people, any means possible. Procreation was performed in labs, but also privately—in different medical offices where people were bred like cattle, for work and for pharmaceutical use. Because of this, it had been years since people had touched one another; there was no need, except during the exchange of money or other essential goods. Kreanga, however, touched people when it was unexpected and, above all, when it was unnecessary. If one of his servants walked by him, he would change his position so that they'd be forced to brush against him with a part of their body I described in my stories: ass, breasts, hands, and so on, those parts that provoked a particular discomfort in people unaccustomed to sex. The reason why Kreanga hung out with me was that it was easier for me to tolerate his touching.

Kreanga requested that I write porn in the first person, of course—that, if possible, he should be the narrator. He hoped that, reading the text, he would identify with that person who thought only about sex, with that insatiable, promiscuous literary character Kreanga.

My little slut, my puppy, I'm hungry for your fleshy tight pussy that lustfully melts for my tenacious cock, gladly receiving it, sucking and nibbling in satisfaction. Your voracious cunt, which I imagine growing wet as soon as you think of me fucking you, which you must satisfy with your fingers when I'm not there, rubbing against the sheets until you come, moaning. You're shy, you naughty thing, and I know you worship dick, and I'll gladly give it to you, just how you want it: rough, all the way inside you. You'll groan and beg, your body slippery as an eel, my cock disappearing between your milky ass cheeks, I won't stop until I finish. I'll fill you, little one, you'll be my happy, dirty girl, you'll ask me to piss on you.

It was so difficult to write, I'd have to pause after each paragraph to get some air. I agonized over every word, reviewing the text to see if what I'd written made any sense. I'd page through D. Elmiger: the testimony of the last woman to experience sexual pleasure. And I'd occasionally have to stop and laugh. Here I was, copying a woman's writing so that Kreanga would feel more like a man. Then I'd continue.

I'll fuck your mouth while your wetness drips down your thighs. You'll beg me to put it in you, before you pass out. Don't worry, I'll satisfy you, your pretty pink animal spreading herself in the heat of passion, ready for my big

cock, slut, you'll moan and beg for it, I'll grab your thighs
and spread your legs until I can see the darkness of your
wet flesh, the slit of your desperate cunt, open and ready,
and I'll enter you with ease, fast, and you'll feel the force
of my thrusting, I'll impale you mercilessly, I'll lie on top
of you and pant: "My bitch, my lapdog, how I love you."

"It's pointless of you not to reply," writes Asja.
I'd fallen asleep and hadn't seen her new message.
"I was sleeping."
"I'm coming over. You'd better let me in."
"Where are the others?" I ask suspiciously.
"At my place, where it's safe. If everything turns
out okay, they'll come too."
"Okay," I reply.
I move the furniture away from the door so my
guest can enter. I'm still not sure this is a good idea,
but I can't keep torturing myself anymore. I've tucked
the hunting knife under my belt. Just in case.
I don't know what day or time it is, but despite
this, I try to calculate exactly when she'll arrive. As
soon as I sit down, I hear someone entering the building. I shudder, terrified. I peer through the keyhole.
My neighbor's home from work. I don't know why
she still bothers—they don't pay her at all. I return
to my chair. My underwear is soaked, like I've pissed
myself.
The last job I had was awful. I was a receptionist
at the main municipal laboratory. The night shift.
That was when I started writing a blog, to stay

awake. I kept it anonymously, but the lab found out anyway and immediately fired me. The management didn't like the topics I covered. It's true, I wrote about genetic engineering, which concerned them directly, but I didn't write anything negative. I never knew what bothered them exactly.

Luckily, I had an apartment left to me by my aunt, so I wasn't worried about ending up on the street. I could no longer find work, though. No one wanted me. Eventually, I became so poor, I tried moving to the countryside so I could grow my own food or at least steal from someone else's garden. That's how I met Kreanga.

They say that one of the upsides to cloning is that the clone can't be distinguished from the original. It seems to me, though, that this would actually be a downside: because of their shared appearance, the same person suffers over and over. A person gets cloned only so that they can be exploited by others. The original ostensibly has the advantage: the copies must be worked to death by forced labor. But how do you know who is the copy? Who is original anymore? Human beings surely aren't. I wrote about this too. Upon further reflection, it occurs to me that perhaps this was the reason for my termination, but maybe I'm just lying to myself; maybe I fell asleep at my desk a few times or they caught me stealing the pills I was supposed to be guarding.

What amazed me, actually, was that Kreanga cloned me not once, not twice, but four times. Maybe he just couldn't stop himself. I'm sure he quickly realized his mistake: every single one of my clones was a person unto herself, and none of us could help him.

At work, I also observed that gender roles persisted even without sex. I say this because the laboratory cloned different people for different jobs. I don't know why; there were no fundamental differences. One has to admit that Kreanga would never have cloned a woman unless he needed her for "special occasions." He'd adopted the prejudices of others: if he was going to achieve arousal, he wanted it to be in the company of a woman, even though he hardly understood, just as I didn't understand, what arousal even was.

While I wait for Asja, I shift uncomfortably in my armchair. My legs are numb from poor circulation. I imagine our encounter, something like the first meeting of Bouvard and Pécuchet. We sit on a bench, holding identical hats, and suddenly realize that the same name is sewn into the lining of both: Asja.

Soon I hear a knock at the door. No doubt she's arrived. I open it cautiously, eyeing Asja, that is myself, and say without thinking, "He did a good job, you look just like me."

Asja laughs. We shake hands and she enters the apartment. She makes a beeline for my chair, which makes sense because, in a way, it's also hers.

"I know where you keep your knives," she says.

I start thinking I'm the clone and she's the original.

They're exactly where she says. She even knows that I was looking for them earlier.

"Well done!" I say.

I feel a strange fear. I can't relax in front of myself.

"What about the rest of the group?"

"Are you nervous?" Asja asks.

"Yes," I confess. "Very."

Asja lolls in the armchair, throwing a leg over the side.

"What should we do about Kreanga?"

"I don't know," I say, "but I have no intention of going back. He's a jackass."

And thus do I finally admit to myself that I've wasted three years of my life in the company of a jackass.

"True, he's stupid, but he's not a bad person. Just lost."

I don't get why Asja's defending him. I listen to what she's saying, but really, I'm watching her. I feel that I'm the one sitting in the armchair even though I'm sitting across from it, but not quite: my guest is merely one of my variants, a person unto herself.

While we're chatting, Asja begins to massage her neck. My neck isn't cramped at all. My legs hurt, but hers are fine.

"We're completely different," I say.

I've interrupted her midsentence, and she doesn't remember where she left off.

"You said it would be better to resolve things with Kreanga in person," I remind her.

"Yes, yes. That's the best way."

"One of you should go. Kreanga will never know the difference."

"All right," Asja says. "No problem."

I stare at my copy: crooked teeth, blue eyes, blond hair; same weight, same height. On the outside, it's me. There's no denying it. While I'm contemplating our surface similarities, my gaze lands on her bare shoulder. Asja is sweating. Her leg is still hanging over the chair. She rubs her neck from time to time, but lightly. Like she's rubbing it just for fun. Her upper lip begins to perspire. I mechanically run my tongue across my lip, as if I could wipe her sweat away.

"Why are you licking your lips?" she asks.

"I don't know."

I can feel that I'm squeezing my own leg too. It doesn't hurt anymore, but I can't stop. Asja throws an arm behind her head, across the chair's edge, and I see her underarm is smooth. I have an overwhelming urge to lick her armpit with the tip of my tongue. I'm not sure if I read something like this in D. Elmiger, and therefore I should replicate the gesture, or if my desire has nothing to do with what I've read. Asja notices my confusion, but doesn't say anything. She returns the hand she placed on the chair to her lap and begins to scratch between her legs. Her shorts have bunched up in her crotch.

"If Kreanga reports us, we'll be captured and enslaved. You have to help us," I hear her say. "I did everything you requested; I deleted you so Kreanga has no way of finding you. Now it's your turn."

I hear her, but I'm not listening. Her voice is muffled; her speech, slow and quiet. My hand is also between someone's legs, I don't know whose, hers or mine, but it's not scratching. It's doing something completely different, something long forgotten. The feeling of a hand's touch can't be expressed in words.

CARNIVORE

When he got on the bus that day, Milan detected the strong scent of raw meat. The woman who was sitting a few seats in front of him, he instantly concluded, was carrying the paper-wrapped treasure in a bag. Tucked in beside it were peppers, an onion, but none of the vegetables corrupted the meatiness of the aroma. He observed her with interest. They got off at the same stop and walked one beside the other. And then came that strange gesture, an unexpected moving hand. The woman slipped him a piece of paper with her address and said he should come over for dinner.

"There will be fresh meat," she whispered, then headed off in the other direction.

Milan touched his genitals, which a moment earlier had brushed against her hand. Not even Geppetto could've whittled better wood. What would he say to his wife? She was consumed by jealousy, and he feared her reaction. But he just had to go to that dinner. Ultimately, he stopped by the pharmacy for some sleeping pills. "No more than two at a time," advised the pharmacist.

"So, three," he said to himself as he climbed the stairs to his front door.

His wife was in a good mood. She didn't ask him where he'd been or what he'd been doing. A miracle! Milan thought. While he ate his meal, his wife talked about her plans for the weekend. She was going to spend it with a friend at a cabin with no phone and wouldn't be able to contact him. He choked.

"No way to call?"

"Right, I won't be able to call. I hope that doesn't bother you."

"Okay," Milan said softly. And then, even more softly, "I'm going to take a walk later tonight. Would you like to join me?"

"No, you should go by yourself."

She didn't ask where he intended to go. Milan was dumbfounded.

"Are you all right?" he asked. "You don't want to know where I'm going?"

"You said you were going for a walk. I trust you."

Milan didn't say a word. He sprawled on the couch and propped up his legs on the coffee table. His wife lay next to him. There was some documentary about herbivores on TV, and he commented that he just didn't understand vegetarians. "Meat is everything," he said, then remembered he hadn't asked the woman from the bus what time he should come over. This rattled him.

"I'm going out to stretch my legs before calling it a night. Not sure when I'll be back, I may stop somewhere for a drink."

"All right," his wife said.

While he made his way to dinner, Milan kept turning around to see whether his jealous wife might be spying on him. He didn't see her. She really must've calmed down, he thought with relief. Still, just in case, he circled the block twice. As he strode along, he remembered how she'd followed him on his way home from a friend's house the year before. It had been dark, and he wouldn't have even noticed her had it not been for a streetlight switching on.

He knocked on the door calmly, as if he wasn't inclined to pounce on the stranger the moment he saw her. A man opened the door. Confused, Milan said he'd been invited for dinner but didn't know the exact time, so here he was. "We're eating at nine," the man replied. "I think you've got the wrong apartment." Milan was nearly brought to tears. All of this was probably just a prank concocted by my wife, he thought, turning to leave. But then another door opened and a woman told him to ring the door with the name Joguncić.

"My neighbor is always eating something, maybe she's the one who invited you," she said pointedly, shutting the door.

Milan sensed that someone was watching him through a peephole, and it unsettled him. Then another door opened, despite the fact that he hadn't yet reached it or rung the bell.

"You didn't say to look for the door marked Joguncic," he said as he entered, disconcerted. "I rang at your neighbor's place."

The woman said nothing. The apartment was practically empty. On the dining room table sat something wrapped in paper.

"Why isn't the meat in the refrigerator? It'll go bad."

"That's not meat," she replied, laughing.

"It's not?" he asked. "I could've sworn it was."

"Take a look," she said, and Milan inched closer to the table to see what she was talking about.

In the paper sack were three apples.

"But that scent I detected . . . ?"

"That was me," she said.

"*Your* meat?" Milan asked.

"Yes, my meat."

Milan drew nearer to the woman. She was petite, and he looked down at her.

"I wanted to bite you, kiss you," he said.

"And lick," she said. "Panthers pick the meat off the bone with their tongues."

"You're right. Where shall I dine?" Milan looked around.

"Here," she said, pointing to the table. "But before that, I should eat something."

The woman pulled out two apples. She sliced

them and then grated a carrot into the same container.

"And the meat?" Milan asked.

"I'm a vegetarian."

Seeing the strange look he gave her, she asked if that was a problem.

"No, not at all. Meat is meat, even if it's vegetarian. It's just that"—Milan's tone became more intimate—"I'm interested to know how you're so meaty then."

The woman laughed, but didn't say anything.

"Can I touch you?"

"Wait until I've eaten dinner, then I'll have my dessert."

"You can't mix sweet and savory?" Milan asked, rubbing his leg nervously.

Again she didn't respond.

"Are you married?" she asked him.

Milan became confused. He'd completely forgotten that he was.

"I am," he said, dejected.

"It doesn't matter. I'm sure your wife is asleep right now, dreaming about something lovely."

Milan went silent. He remembered that he'd forgotten the sleeping pills in his pants, which he'd swapped for these plaid ones he preferred.

"Did you want to put sleeping pills in her tea?" she asked him.

Milan blanched. How did she know? The

apartment, which had looked so empty before, was suddenly filled with the woman's shadow. Calm down, Milan said to himself. She eats plants, not people. Then he remembered what his wife had said to him when he'd forgotten their anniversary the previous year: "Men aren't people, they're weeds."

"Are you a feminist?" Milan asked, frightened.

"Where did that come from?"

"I realized I don't know anything about you."

"Look, I ate my dinner," she said briskly, pushing the empty bowl toward him. "Are you sure you want to talk about me instead of really getting to know me? A dream doesn't last long. Your wife will wake up, and she'll realize you aren't next to her."

Milan looked at his watch. It was past ten.

"Uh, I really should be getting home," he said.

"No, you shouldn't, not if you don't want to. I have a phone. Call her and say you're at a friend's. Make something up."

Milan considered, and reconsidered. The strange woman really was too beautiful, but she also scared him. After his hand had hung in the air for a few seconds, he picked up the phone and dialed his home. No one answered. This unnerved him. Where could she have gone? He tried calling again.

"She's not there," Milan said. "She'd pick up right away if she were. I need to go and make sure everything's all right."

"If I were you, I wouldn't worry."

"Why not?"

"Come this way," the woman said, pulling him by the hand.

A soft light glowed in the bedroom. The closet door was ajar. When Milan got closer, he saw, huddled among the clothes, his wife, bound and gagged, a blindfold over her eyes.

The unknown woman proposed that they tie Milan's wife to the bed and wait for her to wake up.

"Maybe we can persuade her to have a threesome."

"I don't know . . ." Milan shrugged.

"You don't know what?"

"If she'd like you."

The woman laughed.

"Of course she would, I'm just her type. She's lucky you liked me as well," she said, turning toward the closet.

Milan hastened to help. He was no longer afraid of the stranger. He couldn't explain why, but his wife's body had put them both at ease. They transferred his sleeping spouse to the bed, but didn't tie her to it. They sat beside her and waited for her to wake up.

"How long have you been married?" the woman asked.

"Five years."

"That's not so long."

"True, it's not," he said. "I've known myself much longer."

The woman placed her hand on his knee. Milan recoiled.

"Not now, not while Jelena's sleeping."

"Okay."

"I'm guessing Jogunčić isn't your real name," Milan said after a short pause.

"It's not. I rented this apartment to have a place where I could meet my lover."

"You like women?"

"Yes," she replied.

"Then why did you seduce me?" Milan asked.

"Your wife wanted me to."

Milan wasn't surprised. He'd always contended that Jelena was masculine. Rarely had he dreamed of her alone: in his dreams she seduced other women and laid them at his feet.

"How long have you two known each other?"

"Jelena and me? A few months," she said. "I rented this apartment for her."

His wife began to stir.

"There you are, love," she said.

Milan didn't know which of them she was addressing. This was difficult for him, and he left the room. His wife remained on the bed. Her lover followed him.

"Would you like a little rakija?" she asked.

"Sure," he said with relief. He'd thought the stranger had nothing but fruits and vegetables in her house.

"I have some cheese too, if you'd like. It's not bad."

"Okay," he said, gazing vacantly toward the bedroom, from which a little light was escaping.

He turned away to avoid seeing his wife's feet through the half-open door. At least he could do that much.

"Here's your rakija," the woman said, handing him a small glass. "I poured myself some too, so we could make a toast. To Jelena!"

"No, no. Let's toast someone else. Us, for example."

"Okay," she said. "To us!"

"To us!" Milan echoed, as if an "us" really existed.

PASSIONS

For a long time I didn't know whether Vanja was a man or a woman. When we'd pass each other in the hallways on campus, I'd always stare at her shamelessly—looking for a sign that might help me solve the mystery of her gender. When we started hanging out, after we'd met at some student party, I stuttered through my explanation that her name and her physique perplexed me. Vanja joked that she wouldn't hold my confusion against me, because she wasn't exactly sure which team she played for either.

"As long as I'm on the winning team."

"Then you're a woman," I said.

I believed this conversation sealed our friendship. I was convinced we'd grow old together, talking about the same things then that tormented us in our youth, but Vanja went away after graduation and we didn't see each other for years.

It's hard to articulate what went through my mind when I noticed her in the middle of the hotel ballroom. So much time had passed, I needed to close my eyes for a moment. I couldn't believe it was really her. I slowly walked up behind her. Vanja turned around and, without a trace of surprise, uttered the most perfunctory hello. We exchanged a few words, speaking very formally, then said our goodbyes and proceeded along our respective sides of the buffet table. Later I spotted her embracing a man I didn't recognize, which only added to my confusion. I wondered what Vanja saw in him. But then she vanished from my sight.

I knew nothing about *Passions*, the novel whose launch party Vanja and I were both attending. I was told it was good, but I tended to be suspicious of anything I hadn't written myself. One of the other guests, noticeably tipsy, wanted to summarize the book for me, but I luckily managed to escape. The novel had been released pseudonymously by my publisher, and the launch was an important event. But I couldn't care less—I kept scanning the room for Vanja. I chatted with a few acquaintances and periodically inquired about her. No one knew who I was talking about. The conversation returned to the book we were there for, all of us with our full mouths and emptied glasses. Everyone insisted I simply *had* to read it. "You've got competition," they said, patting me on the shoulder.

An hour later, a little unsteady on my feet, I saw Vanja exiting the hotel lobby with the same man and wandering into a nearby park. I set off to follow them. I wanted to find out what they were up to, even though I knew literally nothing about such passions, even those bound in books. I understood, however, that I'd discover nothing about Vanja, not only because it was getting dark, but also because I had no idea what I even wanted from her. I continued walking anyway.

Slowly following the couple, I paused a few times to hide behind a small tree or some bushes—I was afraid they'd see me. I wouldn't know how to explain what I was doing there; I was even surprising myself. Vanja, in the meantime, began to kiss her companion passionately against a tree. Watching them, I couldn't stop thinking about the novel. While I listened to their sighs, my mind wandered to the hotel lobby, to the poster announcing the book. *Passions.* Who was the author? Did I know him? Or was it a her? I glanced toward Vanja, who was making the unmistakable sounds of fellatio, but instead of watching her and her lover, I hatched a plan to blackmail my editor: if he wouldn't tell me who'd written *Passions*, I'd publish my next book somewhere else. I imagined his outrage, how he'd vent to his secretary that authors were vermin—especially women authors, the worst of all!

Even though my literary debut, a collection of essays, had been critically acclaimed, I'd found real success as a novelist, writing about something of which I knew nothing: human relationships. Only then was I taken seriously; only then was there collective acknowledgment that "this one knows what she's talking about!" My first novel was about Medea, who didn't know how to poison her rival Glauce. The sorceress couldn't guess what kind of clothing her husband's new lover might like best—my Glauce wore secondhand clothes from a flea market—even though their taste in men was identical. For some, the obvious message of the book was that men and women couldn't be swapped or discarded as easily as clothes, while others concluded I was trying to revive socialism because Glauce's distaste for expensive garments and reluctance to accept golden gifts saved her life. All of these interpretations were complete nonsense, of course, but my publisher forbade me to say this publicly. I eventually decided to refuse interviews altogether so I wouldn't risk alienating my readers and critics.

It wasn't a coincidence that Vanja had long been the sole person I considered in the superlative. Considered, but never told, because I didn't want Vanja to know just how much I admired her. I can't emphasize enough how deeply I detested conversation with other people; I ran away from them. But Vanja was the exception: I enjoyed her company. I believe I even dreamed of her when I was younger, when our discussions were particularly stimulating. But we hadn't seen each other in so long; I'd lost that feeling of intimacy and reverted to my old hermetic ways. I didn't know how to converse one-on-one, or in a group. I found it all exhausting. "Hell is other people," said a philosopher who was himself somebody's hell. When

I saw Vanja that evening, though, I immediately wanted to grab her by the hand and drag her to some darkened room where we could continue speaking in hushed tones, as relaxed as if I'd never been afraid of conversation, as if I were an expert in the art of the tête-à-tête.

When we'd first met, Vanja and I both had harbored literary ambitions. Despite being a brilliant conversationalist, however, Vanja had been incredibly lazy and never managed to write anything. But as I stood in silence just steps from her, it seemed to me she'd become some other person, someone who could write with great ease. As if, in the darkness of the park, at the heights of pleasure I couldn't understand, she'd transformed into a paragon of accomplished writing. This Vanja surely could've written *Passions*, I thought, almost offended. This Vanja did write *Passions*. I was convinced of my discovery.

When a woman speaks intelligently, it calls her gender into question. Vanja had short, boyish hair, but I never noticed her, or really anyone, below the neck. I didn't know then, and still don't know, what to make of a person's genitals. I've always pretended there's nothing to a person besides their head. Still, it was clear to me that people's attention was constantly split between two anatomical points: the head and the groin. I applied this knowledge in my books and received many letters from readers thanking me for writing in a sincere and intimate voice that "opened their eyes" and "helped them realize something."

Needless to say, my publisher was delighted. I, on the other hand, couldn't have cared less.

Although Vanja's androgyny was stunning, I always found it easier to imagine her as a woman. I'd often catch myself daydreaming about writing books on her behalf. Mostly they'd be genre fiction, especially horror and science fiction. I was certain that Vanja, had she not wasted herself on conversation, would've made a great author.

If I sometimes had an erotic afterthought, it was only while trying to think like her. Vanja was androgynous, true, but I'd never met anyone as sensual and tactile. While we'd be talking, she'd inevitably touch my arm or my leg; these were the only moments in which I allowed others, and myself, such familiarity. At other times, any touch was repulsive and caused me horrible discomfort.

Our separation was hard on me. Vanja got a job offer in another city and accepted it without a second thought. She even bragged that the move was a unique opportunity to put her empty life in order. I took her pronouncement personally and never contacted her again; I even ignored the emails she sent the first few months after her departure. If she considered her life empty, it meant that for her I was also empty, just stale air, unlikely to enrich anyone's life. After a while, Vanja stopped writing to me.

I threw myself into my career in the following years, writing and publishing constantly. Only literature held my attention. Here and there I'd meet people who seemed interesting at first glance, but our relations always remained superficial. No one intrigued me enough to make me want to get to know them better. In my writing I'd often recycle conversations with Vanja, hoping she'd reach out to praise the book, to say how she'd never found a better interlocutor. I wanted her to confess that she missed me, but it was as if the earth had swallowed her up.

Due to the long silence, her appearance at the book launch had come as a surprise. I hadn't told her how strange it was to see her there, and when I'd finally summoned the strength, it was too late—she'd disappeared. It also tormented me that she'd left for the park with her companion, rather than reserving a room at the hotel. I'd never known her to be an exhibitionist. Her behavior confused me. But what confused me the most was the nonchalance with which she'd addressed me. I didn't expect such composure, such indifference. But I was soothed by thoughts of *Passions* and of Vanja as its possible author: maybe the novel was a message for me, the message I'd been patiently awaiting for years.

After Vanja and her friend left, I made my way home. I couldn't sleep. In the morning, I went to my editor's office and gave him an ultimatum. He stared at me blankly. I repeated my question:

"Who wrote *Passions*?"

He remained silent. Confusion passed over his face. Then he said, "Why are you fucking with me?"

His clumsy secretary brought us coffee. I watched

how the girl slowly carried the tray to his desk. I expected her to stumble and fall on her face at any moment. Her hands were shaking, she was so nervous, but the editor paid no attention. Such details didn't interest him. The secretary didn't interest him. He was focused on me. When the girl left, I told him that I wasn't fucking with him, I simply wanted to know. He barked that he didn't understand why I was fooling around so early in the morning, and then asked how my new book was progressing.

"There won't be a new book," I said, "if you don't tell me who's behind *Passions*. Is it Vanja?"

"Vanja who?"

He didn't know who I was talking about.

"For god's sake," he said, "I had no idea your alter ego was a physically separate person. Do you want me to dial your phone number so the two of you can come to an agreement about who wrote the book?"

He continued to speak about *Passions* as a huge commercial and critical success, about the awards I could expect for such a masterpiece. I wasn't listening. I could only wonder how it was possible I'd written and published this book without knowing it.

"When did I send you the manuscript?"

"Three months ago," he said. "I can't believe you're still joking here. You didn't let me call you while you were writing, but I should have. If you keep on denying authorship, I'll have to invent a story about someone hacking into your email and faking your signature on the contract. Didn't you receive the advance?"

The drink sitting in front of me went untouched. I returned home worn out and sleep-deprived. I turned on my computer and checked my email, but the correspondence with my editor wasn't there. My head started to hurt from the stress. I turned out the lights and lay in bed. I shivered with fever. My teeth were chattering. I thought only of Vanja.

I woke up the next morning drenched in sweat. I'd dreamed something unpleasant. I couldn't recall exactly what, even though I usually remembered and wrote down all my dreams. The sheets were soaked. I'd put my cell phone on silent. I had a few missed calls from my editor and a text message from an unknown number. It read: "What do you think of the book?"

I couldn't find the number in the directory, and customer support couldn't tell me who'd sent the text.

"Would you like for us to block the number? So they don't bother you anymore?"

"No, thank you," I said. "It's okay."

Vanja? Why hadn't she identified herself in the text? Damn *Passions!* I needed once and for all to get to the nearest bookstore and buy myself a copy. Back home, I curled up on the couch and began reading. I forgot to call my editor back, forgot to raise the blinds. I read the novel until night fell.

I had only myself to blame. My editor had grown accustomed to my outlandish demands, to my "eccentricity," my refusal to do interviews and literary events. My alleged request that we discuss *Passions* only over email, that he never ask me anything about my book in person, that he refrain from calling me repeatedly to see what I was doing or how I was feeling—surely it didn't surprise him. Commentary about me abounded: how I always appeared in the same clothes, how I wore a ring in the shape of a skull, how I left my house only at night. But the rumors didn't bother me. I didn't fill the papers—it wasn't that kind of talk. I wasn't in danger of ending up in the tabloids. I never got naked in public, never beat people up, although—I must admit—I often wanted to. I'd sometimes wake up with clenched, burning fists. Had I been a poet, I no doubt would've written about such things, but poetry didn't interest me. I didn't read it, and I didn't try to write it. Had my editor been a smarter man, the poetry would've given it away. It would've been instantly obvious that I wasn't the author of *Passions*. I never would've begun a book by quoting verse. Never.

But there it was—serving as the epigraph to "my" *Passions*, a very awkwardly chosen poem by some Japanese writer, some woman by the name of Kasa. Short, but irritating enough to piss me off:

> *To love someone*
> *Who loves you not*
> *Is like entering a temple*
> *And worshipping the walls behind*
> *The wooden statue*
> *Of the hungry devil*

What was that supposed to mean? I hadn't a clue. I couldn't remember if Vanja read poetry. It suddenly seemed very important, maybe the most important element of all.

It turned out that Vanja was still using her old email, that nothing significant in her life had changed—she still used the same phone number, the same email address. Since I couldn't stand talking on the phone, I decided to write her an email. I didn't want to reveal too much. I asked whether she felt like getting together, we hadn't seen each other in so long, blah blah blah—the platitudes piled up. I'd even written *Dear Vanja* at the beginning, which wasn't a lie, but sounded insincere.

It took her three days to reply that she didn't have time, but as soon as she did, she'd get in touch about meeting up for a drink. I was nervous. I wrote back saying I had something important to discuss with her. I should've known she would call me right away. She asked what all this was about, but I didn't say. I proposed we meet that night. She declined.

"I can't meet before tomorrow," she muttered.

"What you can't do today can wait till tomorrow," I said, laughing like a moron.

I tried to prolong the conversation. I had to clutch the receiver with both hands—my palms were so clammy, it was like trying to hold a bar of soap.

"Tomorrow in the main square?" I asked.

"Okay, be there at five. We have a lot of work to do, so I can't stay long."

"We?" I asked.

"Yes, me and my husband."

"I didn't know you were an old married lady," I said, on the verge of tears.

"Don't you just mean married? I'm nobody's old lady."

"Tomorrow at five then," I said, quickly hanging up.

I'd forgotten to say goodbye, see you, or take care. I'd forgotten such formalities. Before my eyes appeared Vanja's husband, that disgusting creature who couldn't possibly deserve her. I'd never met him, but already I hated him. However much I tried, I couldn't recall the face, or even the silhouette, of the man I'd seen Vanja with at the book launch. I imagined him with small, hairy hands and oily skin. Then I started fantasizing that Vanja had actually left the event with a lover. The idea of Vanja lying to her husband brought me a few minutes of pleasure. If it hadn't been for those thoughts, I wouldn't have gotten a wink of sleep.

I slept fitfully. I dreamed of my high school physics teacher, vividly recalling her face, and even more her hair. She'd been a surprisingly intelligent and sophisticated young woman who specialized in electromagnetics and optics. In the dream, I was trying to convince her that physics could actually predict the future, that the task of physics was to show how two bodies with the same charge could attract rather than repel one another. The teacher—whose hair I remembered, but not her name—wagged her finger and fumed that the principles of physics state that positive and negative attract, and negative and negative repel. "And positive and positive?" I asked. Before she could answer, I woke up.

I got to the main square at quarter to five and recognized Vanja right away. She didn't see me. I had to tap her on the shoulder several times before she turned and looked at me.

"Have I become invisible?" I asked.

"No, but you've changed a lot."

"We just saw each other the other night."

"All the same, it's difficult."

"I brought you flowers."

"Thanks," Vanja said, and before I could give them to her, she grabbed the bouquet from my hand.

"What did you want to talk about?" she asked, casually waving the flowers around.

I wasn't sure it was the best idea to bring up the novel yet, so I awkwardly asked if she was happy in her marriage. She pretended not to hear the question.

"Why did you attend the book launch?" I asked, as soon as we sat down at a café.

"My husband was invited."

"Does he know my publisher?"

I was trying to show off.

"Probably. The hotel where the book launch was held is ours."

"It's a shame I didn't get to meet him," I lied.

"Yes, a real shame," said Vanja.

I'd dreamed of this moment, our next meeting, for years, but nothing was as I'd expected. Vanja listened with complete disinterest, as if I were boring her. I imagined she'd start yawning at any minute. I felt humiliated. I knew at once that Vanja hadn't written *Passions*. The Vanja sitting next to me seemed to have been lobotomized. Nothing about her—except her appearance—was special or exciting. She must've been deadened by her husband's money.

"Do you read poetry?" I asked.

Vanja laughed.

"I have no time for literature, only the hotel. The last book I read was over five years ago. Becker or Roethke, I can't remember. You?"

"You know I'm not a big fan of poetry," I replied.

"You don't know what you're missing."

"I know," I said. "I know what I'm missing. I'm not sorry about it."

"You used to tell me constantly that I didn't know how to write. You didn't understand my sensibilities. Maybe if you read poetry, you'd get it."

"I thoroughly doubt it. I doubt it," I repeated. "You talked too much. You used yourself up on conversation like so much soap!"

I paused then, remembering the damp of my hands. Had I clutched the receiver or Vanja? While I sat there, my mouth half open, I noticed Vanja had actually started to yawn.

"Am I boring you?" I asked.

"No," Vanja said abruptly. "Anyway, you wanted

to talk to me about something important. That's why you contacted me. Surely you didn't want to talk about my writing."

"Actually," I said, "that *is* why I contacted you. My publisher released a novel under a pseudonym and I wanted to ask you whether you knew who'd written it."

"I don't know. But it interests me too."

While she said this, she smiled malevolently. At least it seemed like she did. And then she yawned again. Why did Vanja's brain need so much oxygen? I wondered. She must be plotting some kind of stunt. After I brought up the novel, the conversation flowed in a predictable direction. We talked about the books we'd read during our studies, then quickly parted with a promise to meet again for coffee.

"As soon as I'm free, I'll get in touch," Vanja said.

"Okay," I replied, knowing we might never see each other again.

Before we went our separate ways, Vanja briefly commented on an excerpt from *Passions*, like she wanted to show me that she did read something from time to time, despite her claims to the contrary. I never got the chance to say that lying didn't agree with her.

At home I was overcome with exhaustion, as if talking with Vanja had depleted my energy—as if her repeated yawning had sucked up all my strength. Our pointless conversation had aligned her with the others—those with whom I didn't get along.

I lay in bed reflecting on her mannerisms. In the past, she'd used her hands a lot more. Now her gestures were stiff. I concluded she'd lied to me shamelessly about her hotelier husband, because if her husband really had owned the hotel, there would've been no need to go to the park with him; they could've used whatever room they wanted. Vanja, the woman I'd for so long considered in the superlative, was slowly fading from the horizon. I was confronted with a Vanja I couldn't understand. If I had changed, what had happened to her? I pondered these changes until I fell asleep.

Once again I dreamed of my physics teacher. This time we were discussing optics. I complained about how when the eye turns things upside down, the brain sets them aright. I didn't like what the eyes did, I told her in a child's voice. The whole time, the teacher was trying to say she wasn't interested in my opinion, but I wouldn't give her a chance to speak. I didn't like seeing things upside down, but then correctly, I repeated in the dream. It wasn't good for me.

I woke up at three in the morning and couldn't get back to sleep. I was still wondering what had happened to Vanja and whether she'd really given up on literature. I just couldn't believe her. People lied so much and so carelessly that I was certain Vanja had been lying to my face the whole time we were together. Thinking about people's duplicity, I decided to confess to my editor that I wasn't the author of the book—to explain that it was all a misunderstanding.

Of course he'd call me crazy, but I couldn't claim *Passions* as mine, I couldn't attach myself to a book I didn't understand. I read the reviews, all of them positive, everyone commending the book—it was only a matter of time until my editor disclosed my name to the media. The thought of it filled me with an indescribable dread. I shuddered. My cell phone started vibrating.

"You never said what you think of the book," read the message.

"Who is this?" I asked.

"Your admirer."

"Vanja?"

"Not Vanja."

"Who is this?" I asked again.

"Not Vanja," the person repeated.

"Not Vanja" was persistent: I received about ten more messages declaring love for me, asking if I'd liked *Passions*, promising to write another, even better, book, wanting only that I should reciprocate, that I should write something in her name.

"What *is* your name?" I asked.

"Not Vanja."

I sat at my computer and wrote Vanja an email. I said that someone had lied to my editor, telling him I was the author of *Passions*, even though I hadn't written a word of it. Vanja called me that instant, as if she couldn't sleep either.

"Listen, we haven't seen each other in years. I don't know why, out of all our classmates, you decided to contact me. Is it because I have money?" she asked.

"For god's sake, Vanja, weren't we best friends?"

"No, we weren't," she said. "We barely spoke outside of class. You were always terribly shy. If you need money," she continued, "just say so. I know it's hard to live as a writer."

"I don't need your money. I have enough."

"Okay," she said. "Take care."

"Take care."

As soon as we hung up I popped two caffeine pills. An awful throbbing in my temples heralded a migraine. The light began to bother me, and I felt nauseous. I barely managed to drag myself back to bed, climb in between the layers, and gather the little pillows around me. I knew nothing about passions, nothing about people. I knew nothing, in fact, about myself. I knew only that there was Vanja, the image of Vanja, corrected, that my eyes had deceived me, that I'd deceived myself. My head had accepted a distorted picture for years. I'd lived and written with this picture, and now I was supposed to go on without it. Naturally, I didn't know how. Completely broken, I decided to stay in bed till morning.

I'd always identified with Medea: I wrote like a betrayed, rejected sorceress, but in fact, I'd received Medea's gift—her poisonous truth. I was supposed to drape myself in it, to die there where the gift, my phone conversation with Vanja, had transpired. I was supposed to fall like something mowed down, but that didn't happen. By ten the next morning, I was on my feet, and by afternoon, on the road. I went to my editor's office. I had to find out who was behind *Passions*, who was behind the poetry.

My editor wasn't there, so I decided to wait for him. Around me sat young men, writers, poets—I didn't know who they were, I could only assume because they were holding manuscripts and books. His secretary was nowhere in sight, and I grew nervous. The young men waiting with me recognized me, and I suspected they wanted to drag me into conversation. My head still hurt; I wasn't in the mood for tiresome stories. I stood up to move away from them, and began pacing around the reception area. I didn't pay attention to where I was going—I only wanted to disappear—and I banged into the secretary's desk, knocking a book to the floor. I picked it up: a volume of Japanese poetry. Two of the poems were marked with slips of paper. One I immediately recognized, the poem about worshipping the walls of the hungry devil, and in the other the last line was hastily underlined in pen: *my flesh spent with lust.* I stared at the words, looked at them for so long that I completely forgot where I was and why. When I finally mustered the courage to lift my eyes from the page, the young secretary was standing before me. I waited a few moments for my brain to correct the upside-down image.

THE GUEST

When we got to the traffic circle, Aleks stopped the car and looked at me questioningly. I still couldn't tell if we were close. A harsh landscape stretched out in front of us, just gravel and sharp rocks. I shrugged.

"I'm not sure."

"Try again," Aleks insisted.

I leaned out the open car door and grabbed a handful of dirt. At first I didn't notice anything, but then a green pebble revealed itself. I already knew it shone only when placed against warm skin. It went unnoticed just lying on the ground among the other stones and gravel: human touch was what distinguished it.

"We're close," I said.

We drove about ten minutes further, arriving at a hill. I got out of the car. Aleks said goodbye and immediately headed back to the city. I had to continue alone, climb the hill, and wait on the other side for my contact, a young woman who'd agreed to help me. I started to get nervous. I was supposed to find a strange settlement, a wild village, to write an account of Carlyle and his followers. I knew it was dangerous. The army and the police stayed away. Not one journalist had agreed to go there. Someone at the newspaper had remembered I'd written an opinion piece about it, and wanted to see whether my fascination with Carlyle was serious, or purely a publicity stunt.

"I don't know anything about anthropology, about criminal behavior," I had said. "I don't know anything about cults."

"It doesn't matter," the voice on the phone had said.

All I knew about the cult were urban myths and secondhand stories. The paper hadn't told me anything significant. They'd explained that Aleks would drive me to a designated point, but since he didn't know how to recognize the signs—the green pebbles—I would need to take on the role of investigator alone.

"Maybe I should've said no," I said as I climbed up the hill.

It was night by the time I reached the other side. The young woman was there, but she didn't tell me her name, simply took me by the hand. I followed her as if we'd known each other for years.

At the settlement's entrance, she turned and said abruptly, "You'll sleep at my place."

"Okay," I replied.

The streets were cramped, and the buildings appeared unstable, as if they'd been built by children.

Almost all of them were lopsided. The facades weren't painted, just concrete as far as the eye could see. The structures were separated from one another by wire fencing, but all of the fences were full of holes and easy to get through.

"Like the Wild West," I said.

"Just about."

It was very pleasant in her apartment. I was surprised. Everything was comfortably arranged—the bed, the bookcases, the clean bathroom.

"You didn't expect this," the woman said, smiling.

"I didn't," I responded sincerely. "I really didn't."

She showed me to a closet where I could situate myself.

"I only have one bed, unfortunately, and the armchair isn't big enough to sleep in."

"It's all right, this is fine," I said, and lay down, exhausted, at the back of the closet.

I left the door ajar to let in some light. The closet was spacious enough for two people to lie down side by side. The woman had left me a set of blankets, a soft pillow, and a duvet.

"It gets cold at night," she warned. "You should bundle up."

The next morning we had tea. My palms were hot, and I wondered why. I took out my notebook and explained my task to my host: I was writing an article and needed her to answer a few of my questions.

"I'm not sure that's such a good idea," she said. "I like it here, and I wouldn't want Carlyle to banish or punish me."

"Then tell me about the good things."

"That's all right," she said. "I'll tell you, but it's still too soon. I think we should first walk around the village a little, so you can see how everything looks during the day."

While I was getting up from the floor, I accidentally rested my hand on the wall and saw that the place I'd touched had turned green. I did it again a few times and documented the experience in my notes. Once my palms had cooled, the wall was slower to react.

"Strange concrete," I said.

The young woman smiled. She stuck the apartment key in her pocket and we set out on our walk. The sun blazed down on us and I squinted.

"You have bright eyes," she said. "Carlyle loves people with bright eyes, especially green ones."

"I can see the color green is very important to him."

"True. Very important."

"Why?"

The young woman went silent. She quickened her pace.

"How did you end up here?" I asked.

"I was going through a tough time. I'd heard from a friend about a place that was hard to find because it was constantly moving, but whoever managed to find it would never be unhappy again. It took me three years, but it was worth it."

"The settlement hasn't moved in at least two years," I observed.

"Carlyle loves this spot, I don't know why."

"Have you ever considered leaving? What about your family, don't you miss them?"

"I wouldn't want to live anywhere else. It's lovely, and my family is here. I don't need another."

"Everyone says that Carlyle is the leader of a cult."

The young woman laughed mysteriously.

"This place has nothing to do with a cult. Carlyle has no religious agenda, he doesn't tolerate idol worship or people who don't think for themselves."

"Everyone in the outside world thinks you're a cult."

"They have no clue."

She didn't sound insulted. She spoke calmly, as if simply stating the truth.

"Where does Carlyle live?" I asked.

"There," she replied, pointing at a building that looked just like all the others. "When you're ready, I'll take you to meet him."

"When do you think I'll be ready?"

"Are your palms warm?"

"They're hot," I said.

"They need to be burning," she replied, and continued walking.

The sun was still blaring down, and since the young woman wasn't in the mood to talk, I began to think about seawater, which had popped into my mind unexpectedly. I wasn't thirsty, nor had I seen any body of water, but all the same, I couldn't get the image of the sea out of my head. I wondered at myself. I'd always been an exceptionally rational person. The piece I'd written, the one which had caused Aleks and his colleagues to contact me, was a measured consideration of Carlyle. The one thing we could be certain of, I'd claimed, was that the settlement produced a strange rock made up of unknown chemical compounds. All the rest was mere conjecture. The city, the entire country, was buzzing about Carlyle and his cult. There was talk of unusual sexual practices and rituals, of virgin sacrifice, of a golden castle where Carlyle lived. People said all sorts of things, but no one knew the truth. Not one person who'd joined the cult had returned to civilization and spoken out about their experience. It seemed that even those in power, the state officials, knew nothing about the cult's activities. The young woman I was staying with knew how to go to the city for supplies, covertly, in a rusty old car. I guess she'd been spotted. But journalists, being journalists, didn't want to compromise her. She was the sole connection to a completely unknown world, though I'm sure the others would secretly come out as well, to see how people on the other side were living.

As we walked, I observed my surroundings. I didn't see anything out of the ordinary. Cafés, bakeries. A town like any other.

"They threw you in here like a pebble down an empty well," the young woman said out of the blue.

"What are you trying to say?"

"I hope you know that Carlyle won't let you go back."

"We'll see about that," I said.

"You're brave, but that won't help you with Carlyle."

"Tell me a little about him."

"What do you want to know?"

"Everything," I said.

We stopped in front of a building, and only then did I realize that the young woman had been leading me in a circle the entire time. We'd walked around her block.

"Why did we go in a circle?" I asked, annoyed.

"I wanted to see if you trust me," she said. "You're all right. Now we can talk seriously."

We climbed back up to her apartment. Halfway up the stairs I took out my notes; I was dying to hear what she had to say.

"Carlyle has a brilliant sense of humor," she began. "The young men and women he's close with sprout a second pair of ears, like little pig ears. Carlyle calls this process *double sensuality*. His lovers hear when he calls for them with this second pair of ears, and if he rescinds someone's right to be his lover, the pig ears recede back into their heads and disappear. It's not at all uncommon," she continued, "for Carlyle to grant his favor anew and embrace once again a person he previously rejected."

I wrote down what the young woman told me word for word, even though I thought she was speaking nonsense. Pig ears? I attributed her descriptions to a wild imagination and drugs.

"You don't believe me?" she asked, like she could read my mind.

"It's hard to understand what you're saying exactly. This ears-within-ears business sounds pretty weird."

"I know," she said. "But it's the truth." She looked me right in the eye.

"Where are yours?" I asked.

"I haven't gotten them yet. Carlyle and I are still getting to know each other. This honor takes time."

"*Honor*? I wouldn't call pig ears an honor," I said sharply.

The young woman remained placid, as if she hadn't heard me.

"When I get them, you'll see that I'm telling the truth."

I closed my notebook and looked around. A few hours had passed during her short explanation.

"How is it possible for time to pass so quickly?" I asked.

"Anything's possible here," she said. "We'll continue talking tomorrow."

That night I had trouble falling asleep. Nothing made any sense. I was uncomfortable and excited at the same time.

The world is a strange place, I thought. I don't know how I didn't notice it before.

I tossed and turned nervously in the closet. My back began to hurt, but I managed to fall asleep for a short time.

A man's voice woke me. The closet door was ajar, and I saw the young woman talking to a man with his back to me. I tried to adjust myself so I could hear them better, and in the process knocked down a jacket hanging in the closet. The man turned and opened the door. He stared at me in the dimly lit closet as if he could only make out my eyes.

"Get up," he said.

I obeyed.

"What's your name?"

I didn't respond.

"What happened to her hands?" he asked the young woman, not taking his eyes off my fingers.

"She writes," she said, as if that explained everything.

I looked at my hands. They were trembling slightly, but there was nothing unusual about them.

"Bring her with you tonight," the man said, and left.

"What's wrong with my hands?" I asked.

"There's ink on your fingers."

"What's so strange about that?"

"No one uses fountain pens anymore."

"You know," I said, "I didn't sleep very well."

"You can sleep more if you like, but not too long—we'll need to get ready for dinner soon."

"Is there going to be an orgy?" I asked.

The young woman laughed.

"You have a wild imagination. You only think about sex. How do you do it?"

"Well, if there's no orgy, what'll it be like?"

"A typical dinner," she said. "There'll be about twenty of us, no more, since Carlyle doesn't like crowds. Still," she added, "there are certain conventions you'll need to follow."

"What conventions?" I asked sleepily.

The young woman noticed my yawning and said, "We'll discuss it when you get up."

I lay back down in the closet and closed my eyes. I could hear her preparing something in the kitchen. I couldn't fall back asleep. The image of Carlyle wouldn't leave my mind. He was the most beautiful creature I'd ever seen. I needed somehow to reconcile the fact that I liked him. While I was thinking about him, my hands began to twitch. I squeezed them together involuntarily, feeling my palms warm.

You're a rational being, I told myself. You'll soon find some explanation for your physical responses, these burning fists.

I didn't wait for the young woman to wake me, but got up on my own, washed, and headed into the kitchen. No one was there. I heard the rustling of paper in the bedroom. I didn't knock, just entered.

I saw the young woman opening two boxes on the bed. She removed the crinkled paper to see what was underneath.

"Our dresses for tonight."

"You heard me come in?" I asked.

"I did."

"You don't need an extra set of ears then."

"Enough about the ears," she said. "It's time to socialize."

My name was written on one of the boxes. I looked to see what he'd chosen for me. I took the dress in my hands: it was light, semitransparent.

"I'm not wearing this."

The young woman frowned at me.

"You're looking for trouble."

I draped the dress around my neck like a shawl. This seemed like a good compromise. The young woman put on the dress and we made our way to Carlyle's. I gazed at the nape of my friend's neck: she'd tied her hair back in a bun and smelled of lilac.

"Why didn't you choose your outfit for yourself?" I asked.

"Carlyle knows what I like."

"No one knows what you like better than you."

She didn't respond.

"How is it possible that Carlyle's never seen ink before?"

"I don't know," she said.

"He knows everything about you, and you know nothing about him. Isn't that a little odd?"

"Not at all. Carlyle prefers to talk about others rather than himself. In the beginning I'd ask him personal questions, but he kept throwing the ball back to me. Eventually I gave up."

I kept peppering her with questions. "Will there be other writers at the party?"

"I wouldn't call them *writers*. All the artists who come here soon abandon their art and devote themselves entirely to Carlyle. To them, only he matters."

"Nothing matters more than writing."

"No one would agree with you here," she said.

I didn't know what was awaiting me at this dinner, but I'd brought my notebook and pen with me. I wanted to persuade Carlyle to speak with me, even though it was clear he wouldn't allow it. If the young woman was so tight-lipped, I expected him to be even worse.

"That dress looks lovely on you," I said to relieve the tension.

"Yours is prettier. It's a shame no one can see," she said.

We climbed the stairs to the third floor and walked down the dimly lit hallway. The young woman knocked on a heavy metal door. We heard "It's open!" and entered.

The apartment resembled an outlaw's cave, cluttered with various objects. The walls, unsurprisingly, were green and luminous. No other lighting was needed: it was as if the light was built into the rock. At the back of the room stood a large table. No one was seated yet—the host and other guests had been waiting for the two of us.

"Finally!" said one of the assembled. He was obviously hungry.

Carlyle looked us up and down. I wouldn't say he was angry. He frowned slightly, I assumed because of my makeshift shawl. Everyone began to take their seats at the long, luxurious table, and I realized that my place was set directly across from Carlyle's. We were supposed to spend the whole dinner looking at each other.

"What decadence," I said to the young woman.

"I like it," she replied, sitting down.

"I see," began Carlyle, "that our new guest is wearing her new dress thrown around her neck. Isn't that wonderful!"

"Irony! We do have something in common after all," I replied loudly.

The guests looked at me curiously, like I'd just landed from Mars.

"Irony," said Carlyle, "is mankind's best invention."

The young woman kicked me under the table.

"If our guest would be so kind to explain, before we begin our meal, exactly why she is here," Carlyle continued.

"I came to see how you all live, and to write an article about it."

The young woman grimaced; she looked thoroughly afraid. She glanced at me imploringly, as if begging me to stop. But I couldn't.

"You came to observe us like we're some uncivilized tribe?" Carlyle asked.

"No, I came to see your green stones. They're the only thing I'm interested in."

"There will be ample opportunity to discuss them, but first, let's eat and drink."

"Don't worry," I whispered to the young woman. "I'll say I lied to you and you didn't know my intentions."

"I don't know if that will be enough," she said.

The food and drink were delicious. The whole night, I watched the people gathered around the table. All of them were young and attractive. I grew suspicious.

"What's the average age of the guests?" I asked the young woman.

"Twenty-five, thirty? I don't really know."

I avoided looking at Carlyle. I simply waited for him to confront me. After dessert, Carlyle summoned the group to join him in the other room for warm brandy, cordials, and every other kind of spirits imaginable.

"At least I know now that the green has no religious connotations."

The young woman laughed acidly.

"Mint tea," I said at the bar.

I was avoiding alcohol because I wanted to keep my wits about me. Before I managed to take my first sip of tea, Carlyle came up from behind. He placed his hands on my shoulders. A tingling sensation passed through my entire body.

"I hope you enjoyed dinner," the host said.

"I did, it was excellent."

"Tea?" he asked when he noticed what I was drinking.

"I don't like alcohol," I lied.

"What a shame, I like a woman who drinks."

I turned to face Carlyle. I didn't particularly fear him, so I didn't understand why the others were so meek in his presence.

"These people love you. I'm interested in knowing why."

"Because I'm good," he said, smiling.

"I'm good too, but they don't love me. I don't know anyone who'd abandon their friends and family to start a completely new life in my shadow."

Carlyle took my hands in his. With his index finger, he traced the ink stains on my fingers and palms.

"You should've worn the dress," he said.

"I don't like the material. It's too revealing."

We stared at each other in silence. Carlyle kept tracing his finger across my palm, walking it along my head line.

"Are you reading my fortune?"

"What does that mean, reading a fortune?" he asked, taken aback.

"You know, predicting someone's fate?"

"There's no such thing as fate," Carlyle said in earnest.

I scanned the room for the young woman, but didn't see her.

"The walls," I said. "What kind of stone is it?"

Carlyle laughed and released my hand.

"You like it?"

"More than anything," I replied, taking another sip of my now lukewarm tea.

Carlyle excused himself to talk to the other guests. He hadn't answered my question. Finally I caught sight of the young woman. She didn't look happy.

"Carlyle hasn't said a word to me all evening. I'll never get those damned pig ears!"

"I doubt he's mad at you."

"You never can tell with him. He's good at hiding his emotions," she said.

"What makes you so sure he even has them?" I quipped.

After our conversation, Carlyle didn't approach me again for the rest of the night. He simply watched me. We were complete strangers to each other, the only two equals in the whole cave, in the whole settlement.

Alone in the bathroom, I broke off a small piece of stone from the wall and wrapped it in a tissue. The stone wasn't hard, but brittle, more than I'd imagined. I stuck the bundle in my pocket and returned to the party.

As we were about to leave, I returned the dress to Carlyle and thanked him for his hospitality.

"I had a wonderful time," I said.

"I'll see you tomorrow."

On the way home, the young woman told me how Carlyle had praised her unexpectedly.

"And he kissed me on the neck," she said happily. "He didn't seem to mind that you're staying with me."

The scent of lilac had faded; the young woman smelled of citrus now. I couldn't explain how or why. Maybe my nose had tricked me?

Lying in the back of the closet, I unconsciously ran my finger across my palm. The more I thought about Carlyle, the more I liked him.

I pulled the tissue from my pocket. I wanted to gaze at the glowing stones before going to sleep, but I found only gray, ugly pieces of concrete. Then it dawned on me. I placed the concrete on the head line of my palm and watched it glow green once more. My warm skin was the key to revealing the stone's real properties. I contemplated this as I fell asleep.

In the morning, the young woman greeted me with a hearty breakfast. She said Carlyle had come by again, but hadn't wanted to disturb me.

"He asked where you were. He even peeked into the closet to see I wasn't lying."

I searched the closet in panic to make sure the

tissue was still there. All was well—he hadn't touched anything.

"After breakfast, we're going over to his apartment. He wants to speak with you."

"Can I ask you something?"

"You can."

"Does Carlyle have a weakness? Something that gets him to relax and open up a bit?"

"Of course he does," she said. "Women's stockings, with or without back seams, any will do."

I remembered I had a pair in my bag. I didn't know why I'd brought them, but now they were a welcome sight.

"Whenever I leave the settlement, I always buy hosiery. We have everything else here," she added.

I felt uneasy. I obviously hadn't brought stockings to seduce Carlyle, but my wearing them would undoubtedly look like a desperate attempt to ingratiate myself to him. So I could observe and question him further.

"You should put them on," the young woman said.

"Out of the question," I replied. "I'm already warm enough. I'll give them to Carlyle as a gift, unopened, like this. He can wear them himself, if he finds them so arousing."

"As you wish."

She was accustomed to my stubbornness by now; she'd learned to deal with it.

"You know," I said, "I think I'm starting to understand why you like it here so much."

"I told you Carlyle isn't a cult leader. He is much, much more."

When I offered Carlyle the stockings, he looked at me with surprise.

"I heard you like them," I said.

"I like it when someone wears them."

"What did you want to speak to me about?"

"About you, of course," he said.

"What a coincidence—I wanted to talk about you."

The cave looked darker than it had the night before. The young woman sat down in a cozy armchair. I sat too, but in a rigid wooden chair. I didn't want to get too comfortable. Carlyle remained standing. He stared down at us.

"I like what you've done with the apartment."

"If you'd like, you could live in this building too."

"I don't have the money," I said, even though I knew no one ever used money there.

Carlyle and the young woman laughed.

"We only use money on the outside," Carlyle said. "Here it's useless."

"Because you know it's fake?"

Carlyle grew serious. He asked the young woman to leave us.

"Everything around us is a lie," I said, standing.

I touched the wall of the cave and watched the color intensify, its glow shine brighter. Carlyle came up behind me, kissing my neck. I shuddered.

"Doesn't it excite you," he murmured, "the thought of getting anything you want? Anything you can imagine is within your grasp."

"You mean, anything *you* can imagine? I haven't seen anyone else with your gift."

"You have my gift. Look!"

He unfolded my hand and slashed my palm with a knife.

"You cut the skin like tree bark, let the blood flow slowly, and lick as long as you can," Carlyle continued.

But this was hardly vampirism. Carlyle knew the magic of people, the benefits of the living. He lapped at my hand like an obedient dog.

"Imagine something small. Creation should begin with trinkets."

I imagined a marble. No, two marbles. Carlyle gathered my hand into a fist and held it between his palms.

"You have a powerful and complex imagination."

"You flatter me," I said, annoyed.

"Look!"

He opened my hand. In my palm sat two marbles, the same two marbles I'd just envisioned.

"Anything you want," he said. "Anything."

The first things that came to mind were abstract

nouns, inconceivable notions. I wondered whether I could make infinity materialize, or peace on earth.

"And if I wanted something more?" I asked.

"What do you mean?"

"What if I wanted to carry out some dangerous plan?"

Carlyle grew pale. I'd brought him to his limit.

"You didn't know what ink was, what palm reading was. What if I created something that you didn't even know existed?"

Like a confused child, Carlyle begged me to explain.

"What if I could, at this very moment, conjure something horrible in my mind and then make that same thing happen? I could destroy your village, kill all your people."

"That's impossible. The human imagination is limited. Work with what's already here. After all," Carlyle added, "I can answer your threats with equal force."

I looked at the two marbles—they were perfectly round. I hadn't made a single beginner's mistake. I was certain my buildings would stand straight, not lopsided like Carlyle's, but I didn't want to tell him that. It seemed to me that he'd made a mistake in divulging his secret. How did he know he could trust me?

"You're naive," I said. "If two of us exist with this power, there must be others."

"Don't you see?" He laughed. "It's just us—there's no one else."

What I heard Carlyle say then was staggering to me. The army had known about my gift before I did. They *had* tossed me to the bottom of a well like a pebble, just to see whether I could get out.

"They need you," Carlyle said. "They're running out of drinkable water, fuel, natural gas."

I looked at him, my fists clenched. They were beyond hot now—smoke poured from them, finally bursting into flame, illuminating the farthest corners of the cave. I stood in the middle of the room, thinking only of incinerating myself and everything around me.

I knew what awaited me if I returned to civilization. The army would exploit me, the doctors would examine me. They'd completely use me up. My hands would carry out the desires of others.

"A world that can imagine only the material shouldn't exist," I said angrily. "I'll raze it to the ground!"

The marbles slipped from my hand and rolled toward Carlyle's feet. He bent down and picked them up.

"What an article that would be . . . but there'd be no one left to read it. Are you really so eager to have everything burn?" He paused. "You can't rebuild a world that's been reduced to ashes. Believe me, I've tried."

I understood then. His buildings were slanted because they were supposed to be. His dresses were transparent because that's what he was used to. He'd come from a place where no one wrote using ink, or practiced palmistry. The head line didn't serve for predicting fate, but to change it—to transform things from small to large, from material to conceptual.

I looked at the guest and realized why green light emerged from everything we touched. It was the same green dwelling in me, and from me creation sprouted, like small blades of terrestrial vegetation. People could disappear, but everything else had to remain intact.

HEADING WEST

In the children's room, on the floor, sit two sisters, playing. There are no toys around them. The room is disorderly, dirty. They make all-too-familiar hand movements—they stab at something in front of them and then bring it to their lips. It quickly becomes clear that the girls are playing lunch. There's no food; they are only pretending to eat.

"Mmmm, how delicious!" says one of them.

"Mine's even better!" her sister declares.

They're not imagining gourmet cuisine, just ordinary chicken and potatoes, a bit of soup, a warm roll, and, mostly likely, fruit, cakes—things they haven't seen in a long time. One of them closes her eyes.

"When we get there," she says, "I hope Mama takes me out for cake right away."

"I'll go with you!" her sister says. "And Papa should come too."

In silence, the sisters continue to dine on imaginary food while we hear their stomachs rumbling from prolonged hunger—first the older one's, then the younger one's.

Their parents sit in the adjacent room, crying. They cover their faces with small pillows to muffle their sobs so the children won't hear. They've used up the last bit of meat; only beans are left, but they have nothing to cook them in. Their eyes are red, swollen from crying. They're draped in a dirty blanket. There's no water: they can't wash anything, not even their faces.

For days Mama carried around a single egg to make pancakes for the children, but it eventually spoiled. Now they have none. They no longer have electricity either; they warm themselves by a fire they light in the middle of the living room. When there's no wood, they use books. Each time, Mama cries while watching the books burn: she assiduously collected them for years to have something to leave the children. Now they're slowly disappearing, one by one. Instead of being devoured by curious children, they're being devoured by flames.

"Don't worry, Mama," the little girls assure her. "We've already read them all."

And they weren't lying. After a while, there was nothing else to entertain them. Only books. They would sit by the fire and read. Mama explained that those books were *heavy*, that they were only for adults. But the children didn't understand. They took her words literally.

"They're not heavy—look how easy it is to carry them."

The family has been slowly preparing for a trip.

"When are we leaving?" the little girls ask every now and then.

The parents fall silent.

"We need to say goodbye to the neighbors," Mama says softly.

The only remaining neighbors are old and exhausted. Two little grandmothers on the first floor, so bent over that one of them can touch her nose to her knees. The girls often wonder how it feels to be in that position all the time.

"She can't see our faces, how does she know who she's talking to?"

"She can recognize voices," the other sister replies.

On the floor above them, both apartments are empty, and it's like that all the way up to the tenth floor, where an old couple whose children left a few months ago still resides. Their children sent home a little money, but the old people have nowhere to spend it. They stuffed the money into pillowcases to make them more comfortable.

"Do you think they have hair salons there?" the younger sister asks while intently chewing the air.

She touches her hair. She'd like to have curls that fall to her shoulders. Sometimes she dreams of having hair all the way down to her bottom.

"Definitely! They have everything there," the older one replies with an equally full mouth.

"Will Mama take us to the hair salon to get our hair done?" the younger girl continues her line of questioning.

"Of course she will. It would be stupid to walk around all ragged and dirty when we don't have to."

The parents worry they won't make it until the following weekend, when they're finally supposed to depart. Their parents have died: Mama's father, Papa's father, Mama's mother, and then Papa's mother, in that order, all in the space of a year, all from great privation and suffering. There is nothing more to keep them there; they need to help themselves and their children, to embark on a journey no matter how afraid they are of what awaits them.

Papa often squeezes Mama's hand in a show of support: together for better or for worse.

"But everything just gets worse," Mama says when she feels Papa's grip.

In the morning, they find a humanitarian aid package in the torn-up, deserted street. They're over-joyed. They divide it up evenly, giving one part to their hunched neighbors, another part to the elderly couple. Then they look at what they have to share among themselves.

Unfortunately, the canned meat has been opened already and is full of worms. It's inedible. The cookies are all right. Powdered milk, powdered eggs—everything that's not perishable seems fine—but there's no water. They'll need to find some. The city's infra-structure is completely destroyed, the water supply inoperable. Before fleeing, some people constructed makeshift wells. Maybe there's something there.

The whole city is covered in a layer of dust. Papa

often reflects on this. He was a chemical engineer, Mama a literature professor. They had a nice life. They imagined it could only be better for their children, but they were wrong.

"You never know," one of the little grandmothers says. "Life is unpredictable."

The other old woman nods in agreement, but because she's bent over, no one sees.

"We've suffered," she adds. "But there's no use despairing. The dinosaurs didn't survive, and they were enormous. We're tiny but resistant, like cockroaches."

The parents smile at their comments, but there's really nothing to smile about. It's difficult likening young children to cockroaches. Children aren't resistant to anything. When Mama and Papa look at their daughters, they see butterflies with short lifespans, not cockroaches. Or two hummingbirds, as they sometimes call them—not knowing that birds descended from dinosaurs, that birds survived what even cockroaches perhaps couldn't.

From one day to the next, the children would eat their imaginary lunches and dinners, their abundant breakfasts and brunches. They'd open their bags and pretend to take out apple cakes, pineapple cakes, chicken, peas, mashed potatoes—everything they'd once loved to eat, everything they'd once eaten for real. Sometimes the girls would eat their imagined meal so quickly and voraciously that they'd begin to hiccup. They'd wash down their food with pretend lemonade and fruit juice. The pulpy kind, especially good and nutritious.

The days passed so slowly they felt like years. Toward the end of the week, Mama began to pack. She prepared three backpacks: two large and one small. She fastened necklaces around her older daughter's throat—gold, the most resilient and solid of all the elements. She adorned all her own fingers with rings. The rest she hid in her bag. She didn't want to show the driver everything right away, concerned that the smugglers would get greedy and raise the price for the trip to Ancona.

"We don't have much," she told the neighbors. "I don't know if it'll be enough."

"They're humanitarians, they'll be sympathetic," the women assured her. But no one really knew.

They'd heard stories about migrants who'd been thrown into the sea when they didn't have enough. And even without gold around their neck, a person was heavy enough to sink.

Just before their departure, Mama went to throw Zola's *The Belly of Paris* into the fire because there was nothing else to use for kindling. This time, the children cried instead of their mother. The food in that book had been a great consolation: they could no longer see plants, vegetation, anywhere. All that chicory, those bunches of spinach, celery, huge heads of cabbage, artichokes, leeks, red onions, tomatoes . . . The list went on as Zola enumerated, and the children along with him.

"Mama, don't!" the little girls begged. "Please, please don't!"

Ultimately, instead of Zola, she tossed an old photo album into the flames. The little girls carefully placed *The Belly of Paris* in their backpack.

"Celery, pumpkin, onion, cabbage," recited the younger sister, sweeping her hand across the novel's stained cover.

Food had taught her to read and speak.

They needed to bid farewell to the neighbors somehow. The parents were anxious. They didn't know how to tell the old people they were finally leaving.

"Who will take care of them?" they wondered, though they knew the answer.

They knew their departure meant imminent death for those left behind. The aid packages were coming less frequently, and getting smaller.

"We're leaving tomorrow," Mama finally told the neighbors. "They're coming for us at eight."

"We wish you luck," the old women replied. "There's no life left here anyway."

It was harder for the old married couple to accept. Everyone cried.

"Give our love to our family, if you see them," they said.

"We will," the parents lied.

At eight in the morning an armored SUV pulled up in front of the building.

"Get in," the men in the front said impatiently.

The family climbed into the vehicle in silence. As they left the city, the parents didn't look back. The children, however, turned around here and there to see how the skyscrapers looked from a distance. It seemed to them that the whole city was hunched over like the two old women in their building.

Mama immediately handed over two rings, a necklace, and a pair of crystal glasses to the men. They looked satisfied.

"Will there be enough room for everyone?" Papa asked.

"There will be," the driver replied.

He had a strong accent.

"Where are you from?" Mama asked.

"Senegal."

The parents didn't speak French, so they spoke to the foreigners in English. The men weren't unkind. They gave the little girls an apple, which helped.

The SUV deposited them at an unrecognizable location, indistinguishable from what they'd managed to glimpse through the car windows. They needed to wait there for a bus carrying the rest of the migrants. The Senegalese men drove off.

Near them, on the muddy road, about ten more people were waiting for the bus. Everyone looked frightened.

"Mama, who are these people?" the older daughter asked.

"People like us," Mama said quietly. "People who want a better life."

It grew dark. The bus still hadn't arrived. The adults got acquainted, chatting with one another, but the children were shy. Their faces were dirty; they looked like little monsters. The girls heard their parents talking with the parents of other children, but they didn't dare do the same.

"They said we're going to the west coast on a big boat, but I don't believe anything until I see it with my own eyes," one of the adults said.

"You're right," Mama said. "Nothing is certain."

"And food? Will there be food?" a small woman who stood behind the children inquired.

"They promised there would be," Mama said.

The children feared that west coast and that big boat. Some of them had never seen the sea.

When the bus finally came, there wasn't enough room. A fight broke out, but eventually was resolved. The women and children took the seats, and some of the men remained standing. The younger girl sat on her mother's lap, the older on her father's—this was necessary, otherwise Papa would have had to stand too, and the trip was long. He wouldn't have been able to stay on his feet.

There were no checkpoints; they drove without stopping. The landscape looked eerie at night. The road was full of potholes. There was virtually no vegetation, as if a large foot had flattened everything growing on the earth in a single step.

"Mama, why is everything so black?" her little daughter asked when she awoke.

"Because nighttime came."

"But when it's daytime," the little girl continued, "it's still dark. Why?"

Mama didn't know what to say. She hugged and kissed the child. After a while everyone fell asleep, lulled by the steady rocking of the bus. Sometimes, when they drove over a particularly large hole in the road, the parents would jerk to consciousness, only to doze off again. Time passed; no one knew how long. The children were peaceful, even the youngest. No one cried.

"Ancona!" someone finally shouted.

Everyone opened their eyes as if waking from a hundred-year sleep. A heap of rusted iron, wrecks of old ships—they had arrived. The big, dilapidated port stretched out in front of them. The driver laughed, pleased that everything had gone so smoothly.

"Nice guy," commented one of the migrants.

The "boat" was really just a desperate-looking dinghy, *Marina* written along the starboard side. The parents grew anxious.

"This is worse than a raft," Papa said, but not loudly enough for anyone to hear.

"There's room for everyone," the driver boomed. "Don't worry, *Marina* has transported all your friends, relatives, neighbors. You're not the first."

"Who's the captain?" Papa asked.

"I am," the bus driver declared.

The people looked at one another.

"Don't worry, I know how to fly a plane too," he reassured them.

The little girls regarded him with amazement. Maybe he'd been the one who'd air-dropped those aid packages, the dry cakes and salty scraps of meat.

Everyone quickly pushed into the boat's cabin. There was almost no food or drinking water. It reminded the little girls of the damp basement in their building.

"*On y va!*" they heard one of the two crew members say.

Soon Ancona was just a tiny dot on the horizon. As the European mainland disappeared, the migrants' fear grew.

"Papa, who lives in Africa?" the older daughter asked.

"Different kinds of people," her father replied.

"What are they like?" she pressed.

"Good. These are the people who are going to help us."

"And how will they help us?"

"They'll give us food and a place to sleep."

The boat rocked; the sea was rough. Many of the passengers kept going up to the deck to vomit. When the boat's pitching was especially violent, the younger daughter quietly recited passages from *The Belly of Paris*. With each crash of the waves, the little girl would enunciate: *cabbage, carrots, tomatoes*. As if by speaking the words aloud, she could fill her mouth with all those vegetables instead of the stifling air. Only this soothed her.

"Will they give us cake?" she heard her sister ask their father.

"Surely they will."

"Because they're good people?"

"Yes, because they're good people."

"And are we good people?" the little girl asked.

"Of course we are," her father replied.

After some time, one of the crew members—a Moroccan, if they'd understood him correctly—came below deck carrying a bag. He requested that each passenger pay whatever they could. Mama gave him the two necklaces she'd taken off her older daughter's neck. The girl began to shake with fear.

"Think of something nice," Mama told her.

But she couldn't.

"Everything will be all right," the parents repeated to their children.

To prepare for the trip, the little girls had memorized all the African countries and capitals—the only thing they knew how to recite better was food. Had one of the passengers asked them the capital of Senegal, they'd have been impressed, but all of them sat in silence, their heads tucked between their knees. Everyone wondered what that West looked like, what life was like there. Could it really be so much better?

The waves pounded the boat on all sides mercilessly—as if they wanted to turn the passengers' world on its head.

THE UNDERWORLD

I.

The return trip to Mars was always tough for me, and thus I postponed it for as long as possible. I didn't like breathing the artificial air. I so rarely got to return to Earth, my birthplace, using the false papers Lev Soldo had obtained for me. I loved it here: I knew exactly where to eat well, where to get a haircut, where to get drunk. But on Mars I didn't know a thing. The restaurant I frequented there was open around-the-clock and it was always full, as if no one ever slept.

"I hate Mars!" I'd repeat constantly to the waitress, who would tune me out. Why would she have bothered to listen when she thought the same herself? She'd just wave her hand in irritation and tell me to be quiet. I'd asked her once what she wrote, where she was from.

"Stories. France," she'd said curtly, continuing to wipe down the counter.

Lev Soldo was waiting for me between the statues of two politicians, pacing back and forth in small steps because they had been set so close to each other. At one time two writers had stood in their place, but they'd been sent to Mars with the rest of us. Moving had been difficult for me. It had taken me a long time to get used to the stronger gravitational force: my muscles had atrophied despite all the precautions I'd taken, and I dragged my feet along the ground slowly, trying not to fall. Soldo ran up to me and supported me under the arm.

"How was your trip?" he asked.

"Terrible."

"Did you take that decrepit little ship again? What's it called?"

"*Doloroso*," I said. "The captain's a good guy, just a bad pilot."

"How'd you pay him?"

"I gave him a book. He knew it was illegal, but demand is high. He'll make good money on the black market."

We sat in a café. Soldo told me that some important things had happened in Parliament, that the decision to erase us from the historical record was being reconsidered, but he wasn't sure whether they had the necessary majority. He brought his lips close to my left ear as he spoke.

"You can't stay here much longer. They've ramped up enforcement since capturing that Lithuanian writer last week. You know they're monitoring and recording everything. Someone's bound to recognize you."

I lied, saying I'd return to Mars in seven days, when in fact I planned to stay here for at least another two weeks.

"I know you're lying," Soldo said. "Trust me, you don't want to get caught."

In my old apartment, which remained uninhabited, I found some of my things in a box on the floor. There was a table tennis trophy, old photos from a book launch that had escaped the police's attention, a pair of towels, and a broken watch. I found a silver necklace engraved with my initials behind the radiator: a gift from my uncle for my twelfth birthday, if I remembered correctly.

The bed was still where I'd left it. The dresser had been thrown out; the kitchen was completely trashed. I began to feel nauseous. The radiation on Mars was, they'd explained, closely regulated, but I didn't believe them at all. I even suspected that the radiation detector they'd given us was defective. I had frequent headaches and bouts of nausea, both on Mars and back here on Earth, but maybe these were just symptoms of my nostalgia, my desire to come home and stay for good.

I sat on the bed and emptied my pockets. In one was a crumpled flyer printed with the phrase *Earth may not be flat, but space is.* I laughed. Earth *was* flat; we could see from Mars how flat it was.

All of Earth's literary refuse had been relocated to the Red Planet. One day, with no explanation, writing had been proclaimed the greatest evil to have befallen humankind, and all literary works and the people who'd produced them had been banished to space, to colonize a planet where there was nothing but desert sand that swirled around you the second you set foot on it. The rocks were beautiful, but with no one to throw them at, they too had eventually become unbearable.

I'd always thought that many people were writers, but I soon realized how few of us there really were. Some writers, maybe because of this, had anticipated their downfall and dedicated themselves to other things. Many, in fact, had suddenly begun to speak about their craft like it was an illness that could be cured. The most rabid anti-literature zealots were yesterday's passionate readers. I couldn't understand what had happened to everyone, what evil spirit had possessed them. Lev Soldo had tried to explain that demons had nothing to do with it, that they weren't possessed, that if they'd actually been so receptive, whatever ideas they'd read would've changed them for the better. But he was notoriously misanthropic—for him, everything people did was awful. It couldn't be otherwise.

Authors who'd been captured were given a chance at exoneration if they promised never to write another word. Many had agreed to this, but some had pointed out the impossibility of making such an oath, given they'd have to sign the document itself.

"And that's writing, isn't it?" one author had noted.

Despite feeling relieved during my brief visit home, I still couldn't sleep without pills; I couldn't relax. Both on Mars and on Earth, whenever I lay down in bed I felt like I'd piss myself—I didn't trust my body anymore. I'd lost all faith in my urinary, nervous, and endocrine systems. When you live on a hostile planet, everything is a reminder of your weakness, the vulnerability of your organism. Like you're sleeping inside a trap.

On Mars I'd met an interesting writer, Alan Lemke. He'd been living in Canada when the deportations began, but his accent had led me to think he was German. He told me that he couldn't read anymore, that books sickened him. And he wasn't the only one. Mars was full of bookstores, but people rarely visited them out of a desire to read. While in bed, I thought of Lemke, of his claim that on Earth there would no longer be any writing worth reading, and that the same thing would eventually happen on Mars. We'd debated this briefly, but I knew he was right. One book I constantly read was the correspondence of Boris Pasternak and Ariadna Efron. It did the best job of describing our situation.

Food and supplies were sent to us whenever Earth and Mars were closest together—that was the cheapest way. We'd managed to convince some of the suppliers to smuggle us a few things, on smaller ships that used less fuel. We paid in local currency that was basically worthless on Earth, and in books, whose value had increased exponentially since they'd been banned there.

I watched the moon for a long time, the patches of light and dark I'd grown up with. I waited for sleep to come.

When I finally fell asleep, I dreamed again of Mars. I dreamed that the Red Planet was losing mass at such an alarming rate, much more than its usual kilogram or two per second, that it was literally crumbling beneath my feet. Eventually I stood balanced on a planet the size of a tennis ball. Even in my dreams, I was on unstable ground. I woke up with a start, terrified, and it took me some time to remember where I was. There was no water to wash myself with. Maybe Soldo was right, I thought. Maybe it was time to go back.

I walked around the city with my head down. I resented the crowds of people. Some writers who'd been "cured" had become important officials. It would be horrible if they recognized me, I thought, so I hung my head even lower.

Lev Soldo and I had planned to meet at eight that night in front of the Veronika general store. It was Sunday and the store was closed. He was a few minutes late. As soon as he arrived, he pressed a roll of crisp bills into my hand.

"I can't take this," I said. "It's too much."

"You have to. I don't want you always rummaging for books to sell."

I didn't argue further; I needed the cash. I put it in my pocket.

"Remember how we used to talk all the time about how stupid humans are?" he asked.

"I remember."

"And it's still impossible to talk about anything else. That's how inexhaustible it is."

"It's too much," I said brusquely.

We were sitting on the grass in a nearby park. The benches there had light sensors that could expose us if we weren't careful.

"How are you sleeping these days?" Soldo asked.

"Not well," I said. "I'm plagued by nightmares."

"What do you dream about?"

"Mars disappearing, disintegrating."

"That's all?" he asked. "How is that a bad thing? I thought you hated Mars."

"If Mars were destroyed, I'd have nowhere else to go. I have no other options."

"You could always repent," he said. "That Lithuanian did."

"I can't give up writing."

Soldo looked at me knowingly.

"When was the last time you wrote something?" he asked in a serious tone, as if he were inquiring about my health.

I thought about it. Three or four Martian years.

"I don't remember," I said. "A long time ago."

We sat in the dark. Time passed quickly. I'd forgotten how quickly time could fly.

"*Doloroso* takes off in four days. I think I'm going back then. It's time."

"Smart," he said, lying back on the grass.

We gazed at the celestial bodies above, which I didn't find particularly exciting.

"Just don't ask me to guess which constellation is which," I said.

"I won't. I don't know either."

Both of us were actually looking at Mars. We could identify it easily, and couldn't stop staring at it. My gaze wandered now and then to the full moon circling above us. It seemed like it might fall on our heads and crush us at any moment.

That would be a pleasant death, I thought.

Mars was really just an abandoned urban development project. No one had said why the corporations had left the hotel complexes, the residential and business sites, half-constructed. Everything had originally been designed for the kind of travelers who already know exactly what to expect before they set off on their trip. I'm talking about truly unimaginative people. The places they dream of visiting probably resemble the places where they live, just slightly farther away. Eventually, all those half-finished buildings had been left to us authors, and their poorly insulated bedrooms had been filled with books and manuscripts overnight. Upon arriving, I'd tried to find my own works, but the arrangement was so haphazard that I'd quickly given up. I complained to Soldo.

"You can't find anything anymore. The books are lost among the other books."

He seemed to feel genuinely bad about it.

"I always read dystopian fiction carefully," I ranted on, "but it never occurred to me that I'd actually experience it one day."

"I'm planning to visit you on Mars soon," he said, changing the subject.

"I can't wait!" I exclaimed.

He was supposed to travel to Iceland the next day.

"I'd offer to let you stay at my place tonight, but you know I can't really accommodate you," I said.

"I know."

For my return trip to Mars, I pleasantly surprised the captain with a large payment, using both money and a book he'd requested: a poetry collection by a famous Russian author. Poetry collections and anthologies were of special value because of how popular they were with young people. What the kids did with those books I didn't know and, to be honest, I didn't really care.

When we landed on Mars, everything was desolate as ever.

"This is what the apocalypse would look like on Earth," the captain remarked.

I went to see the Frenchwoman at the restaurant straight away. She asked how things were on Earth, and I lied, saying they were great. I had an energy drink and then headed home. And there, just as on Earth, a bed was waiting for me, and a room full of trivial things crammed into tattered boxes. I turned around, surveying my space: I had an apartment, but I was homeless.

Showering didn't help. The water was incredibly hard, and I felt like I was scrubbing my skin with gravel. I knew I should start looking for the books I could use to buy food and clothes, but I decided to lie down and rest from the trip instead.

My body was adjusting more easily to Mars, but the same couldn't be said for my dreams. When I managed to fall asleep for a little while, I was confronted with more nightmares. I think this was due to my chronic depression, my somber disposition on Mars. (Lemke had joked that they'd sent us to Saturn by mistake.) After all, Mars, which had seemed so fascinating on Earth, had become nothing more than a death sentence: dry ice everywhere, a completely inhospitable environment. The frozen geysers at the South Pole looked like intricate webbing from far away, but on the ground, everything became simply monstrous.

As usual, that night I dreamed that Mars was vanishing beneath my feet. Then I woke up suddenly. I hadn't dreamed of the usual crumbling. Rather, something had peeled off my skin. But I couldn't think about this too much. I got up and quickly washed and dressed. I owed a rice merchant a book I still needed to find, to get money for my next trip.

I took a half-hour break, sitting in the enormous library. The lighting was poor, like no one had imagined people would actually read there. Occasionally

I'd encounter other authors who were searching for something in the dense shelves and piles. We were constantly sneezing, our eyes tearing up from the dust.

To Die By One's Own Hand was the book I was looking for. I found it funny that the merchant wanted that particular volume, but he'd insisted. He wanted the English edition, but I could only find a Croatian translation. I didn't worry too much about it; Soldo had given me enough money to cover the next few months' expenses.

Searching further through the titles that were easier to sell, I somehow knocked a thin book titled *Mars* to the floor. I took it home. There was practically no text—it was mainly blueprints of buildings, or something else? I couldn't really understand what the book was about. There was an author credited, Selena, which I assumed to be a pseudonym, and next to it the number 69 in brackets. A year? I couldn't tell. I immediately called Lemke and asked him to come over to have a look. He agreed.

"This must have something to do with astrology," he said at once. "Selena is a moon. And 69 is the astrological symbol for Cancer."

"What does it mean?"

"That I don't know," Lemke said with a shrug.

"I didn't realize you were interested in horoscopes."

"I'm not. I just know a thing or two about them," he said.

After Lemke left, I thought about Lev Soldo,

the chemistry I was beginning to perceive between us—was that the result of astrology? Such stupid and superficial ideas easily infected people's minds, and I was no exception.

To his credit, Soldo handled my melancholy well. After I'd first left for Mars, I'd become another person entirely. I'd been happy, constantly laughing, when we first met; now I needed a two-hour pep talk just to make it from the bedroom to the hallway. But he acted like nothing had changed. I was grateful.

I started planning where I'd take him once he finally visited. To the Olympic peaks, the Lunar plains, Prometheus, and, of course, Utopia, which I found especially nice. We'd visit lots of places, and see how depressing what people had built on Mars was in comparison to what they'd found there. I was excited to finally have company—but as soon as I started thinking about the Martian landscape, I couldn't help but also think of the thin atmosphere, the dusty and toxic air. The thought made breathing more difficult, and I was seized by panic.

While I waited for Soldo's impending arrival, I spent a lot of time with Lemke and Marina Vojtov, a poet, but our conversations were always filled with grief. We recalled how the censor's office in Iceland had wiped all literature from the face of the Earth with a single mandate. And we always arrived at the same conclusion: that literature was truly dead. We didn't know what else to do. We performed our other jobs mechanically, like labored breathing. The

Frenchwoman wiped down the counter, Marina maintained plumbing systems, Lemke worked at the port, and I . . . I sat at home and lived off Soldo's money and resold books on the black market.

"Have you written anything lately?" I often asked Marina.

Before she could even open her mouth to speak, Lemke would shake his head and answer, "You know she hasn't. No one writes anything anymore."

But that wasn't true. Some young man was taking a census of everyone living on Mars because he wanted to carve the list into one of the walls of the unfinished Imperial Hotel. Everyone laughed at him.

"The dead don't erect monuments to themselves," Lemke commented.

The monument didn't interest me, so I showed everyone the book I'd found. One of Lemke's friends, I can't remember his name, thought the sketches depicted a sacred structure of some kind.

"I'm not entirely certain," he said, "but it seems that this marks a prophesied place for a magic ritual." He traced part of the drawing with his finger.

"Perhaps," I said, not yet realizing that I was holding the book upside down. "Anything's possible."

When Lev Soldo finally arrived, I wasn't up to hosting him. I wanted to send him off to wander around alone, or to hang out with my Mars friends. He refused. So I showed him the book. He regarded it with surprise.

"Where is this from?" he asked.

"I found it."

"Where?"

"I don't remember anymore."

I was tired. Soldo had brought me more sleeping pills, the kind we couldn't get on Mars. As I swallowed them, he took the book and began leafing through it. The last thing I heard was the turning of the pages and the rustling of the pillow he was leaning against.

2.

There's a preconceived notion that if you don't wear a protective suit in space, you'll get the bends and explode from the decompression. We get bloated, it's true, but we don't explode. All the liquid in our bodies seeps out from every possible orifice. We lose consciousness. We die in thirty seconds.

It was the first thing on my mind, that kind of death, as I emerged from my drug-induced sleep. My face was swollen, my hands too.

"Are you all right?" Soldo asked.

I wasn't sure.

After I'd found the book called *Mars*, I'd begun dreaming of a smooth, curved metallic substance that would change shape in my presence. The thing would tighten and release. It seemed to be gesticulating, beckoning to me. This time the dream had gone further. When I approached the substance, it at first reflected my form, and then began to assume it. Eventually it turned into me.

Plush materials like velvet retain the impression of the wearer. I don't remember who exactly wrote that, but it's true—plush remembers best. Because of this, I wore only velvet dresses and cloaks on Mars: I didn't want to be forgotten. At the very least, I wanted my clothing to remember me. In my dream, however, the metallic substance remembered me better than the velvet did. It remembered everything I'd ever said or thought, which satisfied me deeply when I thought about it in my waking hours.

Soldo had gotten up from the armchair and moved to my bed.

"What is it?" he asked.

"I had a strange dream."

My brief description seemed to convince him of something. He looked worried.

"*Mars*, this book you found," Soldo began, "is the missing piece."

"Missing from what?"

He hesitated. He was holding the book in his hand, clutching it firmly.

"The thing is . . . what you dreamed about actually exists on Earth. You described it perfectly."

"That's impossible," I said. "Not one picture in this book matches my dream."

"True, but I've seen it. And now I've heard about it from your own mouth. This curved substance you've dreamed about—people excavated it when they were digging up Mars, developing it."

Soldo looked at the title page as he spoke.

"It's as if the book found you, rather than you it."

"Maybe," I said. "It fell off the shelf, even though I wasn't anywhere near it. Like it threw itself at me."

I asked him if there was anything else he recognized.

"There are some drawings corresponding to the place where the substance was found, but I've never been there. I only know because people mapped the terrain before they left the planet to you all."

That "you all" was painful.

"The curved substance wants something Earth has no way of giving it," he continued.

"What does it want?"

Soldo wouldn't look me in the eye. He set *Mars* on the floor next to my feet and hugged his knees to his chest.

"Too many people have died," he said.

"How?"

"You don't want to know."

But I desperately wanted to know. I imagined deadly contact, lightly touching the curves with my hand, the quiver of the all-consuming substance. I could envision precisely the shredded human flesh. Even though the thing was very far away, I felt it acutely, as if it were sitting at the edge of my bed instead of Soldo. It was present in the room. It crumpled the space, just like it did the bedsheet I was lying on.

It seemed like I knew more about this curved substance than Soldo did, even though I'd never seen it. It revealed more of its truth to me in my dreams than it had to those who'd had the opportunity to study it.

"Tell me! I want details," I insisted.

Considering how often I thought of death, what Soldo recounted didn't sound all that terrible, but I saw that it truly scared him. Haltingly, voice trembling, he described an annihilation that I found comforting. People on Earth had died of the thing from which those of us on Mars had been spared. Everything he told me sounded like poetic justice.

"You all should return it to Mars."

I didn't know where that assertion had come from. It was like I'd spoken aloud someone else's thoughts.

Soldo looked at me. "The thing doesn't want to leave Earth empty-handed."

"Well, what does it want?"

He pretended not to hear me. I hated when he kept things from me.

"*Mars*," he said, "has two volumes. This is the first. The other is in Iceland."

"How are they different?" I asked nervously.

A hush fell over us; it was like he'd forgotten what we'd been talking about.

"Well?"

"The second volume is a completely indecipherable codex," he continued. "All we've managed to glean from this alien edition is that someone's natal chart is printed at the end."

I knew what a natal chart was, but it seemed foolish to be talking yet again about astrology.

"How does that fit in? Is it the natal chart of the curved substance?"

"No, it belongs to a person born on Earth."

"That could be anybody," I said. "Look how many people are down there."

Soldo went silent again. He was hiding something.

"Many people have died," he said suddenly. "Soon even more will die."

Lev Soldo looked me right in the eye this time. He wanted to see my reaction, but there wasn't one. I didn't feel any compassion for the people I'd left behind. I was sure Lemke and Marina would've reacted similarly. Even the Frenchwoman, although she was usually quite reserved.

What had made us human on Earth had quickly disappeared on Mars. I assumed it would have been the same for anything taken from Mars to Earth. The experience of isolation had changed the substance, as had people's hostile intentions.

"How do you control it?" I asked.

"It's currently at the North Pole, deep underwater. Far from human civilization."

"You switched us out, exchanged us. You brought us up here, and that thing down there. Why?"

"We needed to separate you."

He explained then that a fragment of the codex was written using the Latin alphabet, simple notes scrawled in the margins that could be easily deciphered. They directly linked the authorial imagination, the power of the written word, with the curved substance found on Mars. The author whose natal chart was printed in *Mars* was in fact an instrument that would help the excavated substance transform the Earth and surrounding planets, even the celestial bodies beyond the Kuiper belt. In order for this instrument to pass the initiation phase, they would need to possess the second, Latin volume. The megalomania of Earth's authorities had quickly kicked in—they didn't know where the second book was, but wanted to get to it first. They wanted to rule over space; they believed they could. Some thought that the second book hadn't yet been written, and that authors should be locked up with the books so they could speculate in their writing about the excavated substance without having to be physically close to it. The encounter with the thing needed to happen blindly, through written text. No other way. That's what the annotation said.

"Why didn't they just leave it on Mars?"

"Mars doesn't have the proper conditions for studying it," Soldo said.

His explanation didn't make any sense to me.

I got up from the bed, my plush cloak dragging behind me on the floor. My hands and feet were freezing, like my blood had stopped circulating. My heartbeat was barely audible. I felt an indescribable rage. In the crooked mirror I'd hung above my old writing desk, I saw my reflection. The circles under my eyes were nearly black, my chronic insomnia obvious to anyone. All of my dreams had become sickening visions; I would wake up even more exhausted than when I'd lain down. My face was the face of a stranger, a person who could no longer recognize herself. I'd always been pale, but now I looked transparent.

"This natal chart," I said, "do you know whose it is?"

"Now that you've found *Mars*, we know."

I had my back turned to Soldo, but I could see his expression in the mirror. The difference between our expressions was that his seemed free from suffering. He slept and lived in peace. He hadn't changed at all. My pain hadn't affected him, despite us being close. And then, in the throes of the violent anger coursing through me, I finally realized why.

While living on Earth, I'd blamed my everchanging moods on the moon. I'd attached the entire weight of my humanity, my volatility and mutable nature, to its phases. But on Mars I'd found only two tiny, incomprehensible moons that hardly compared to the one I'd known. I had nothing to rely on anymore, nothing to hold on to. Completely disoriented by the new sky, I'd forgotten how important the earthly one had been to me. On Earth my insomnia was fleeting, provoked by obsessive thoughts about books and people I knew. Now, with no writing, no rest, and no moon on the horizon, I'd lost my identity. I hadn't only lost Earth by leaving for Mars; I'd lost the moon, I'd lost myself.

Lev Soldo approached me from behind and embraced me. He caressed me affectionately, but the meaning of his touch was lost in my foul mood and the plush folds of my cloak.

"In this divorce between us writers and other people," I said, "the moon belongs to us."

Soldo released me. He knew that my relationship with the curved substance ran deeper. The natal chart at the end of the second volume was proof: Mars was ascendant, where Soldo would never be—in first place, in my first house.

Both of us could simultaneously conclude how the thing had found its human half, its shredded flesh. Everything was in its place. Everything except— the moon. In the magic ritual Lemke's friend had glimpsed, the moon would be transferred to the Martian sky. For this theft on Mars a person was needed who had nothing to lose, who was ready for anything. So it had come to me.

"And people?"

Soldo appealed to my humanity.

"What about them?" I asked.

My anger had finally come into its own.

It was clear now that the planet crumbling to pieces in my dreams hadn't been Mars, my home, but rather Earth—a place I would never see again.

AFTERWORD

Asja Bakić is a bold social critic, an outspoken feminist, and a provocative blogger. She published a book of poetry (*Može i kaktus, samo neka bode* [It Can Be a Cactus as Long as It Pricks]) in 2009, and this book of stories, first published in Croatian with the same title, *Mars*, in 2015. She has translated works by Emily Dickinson, Henri Michaux, Alejandra Pizarnik, Klaus Mann, Emil Cioran, and Jacques Rancière into Croatian from English, French, German, and Spanish. In addition to writing at her blog, *U carstvu melanholije* (In the Empire of Melancholy), she was one of the editors of *Muf*, an online magazine. She was born in the city of Tuzla in Bosnia and Herzegovina, and now lives in Zagreb, Croatia.

Until a generation ago, there were very few women writers published within the literatures of what was then Yugoslavia, besides several notable poets and a small group of prose writers, mainly novelists, diarists, fairy tale tellers, and travel writers. During the 1980s, in the years leading up to the outbreak of the Yugoslav Wars—first in Croatia, then Bosnia, and then Serbia and Kosovo—this suddenly changed. A powerful, unprecedented generation of women began writing primarily fiction, but also poetry, plays, and essays lambasting nationalism, domestic abuse, politics, war—some explicitly espousing feminism, all championing women's voices. Whether through their example, the broader cultural context of women writing all over the world, or both, these literatures were transformed. Now, in the second decade of the twenty-first century, it is women whose writing leads the way, offering the most engaging voices and explorations.

While the breakthrough generation of women writers—spearheaded by Slavenka Drakulić, Daša Drndić, Biljana Jovanović, Vedrana Rudan, and Dubravka Ugrešić—has pursued narratives that reflect their lives, often written in the first person and fueled by the outrage and atrocities of the 1990s, Bakić has chosen otherwise. "I have no wish to write about myself or write myself down in countless versions because I have social media and my blog for that kind of writing, and sometimes it is all a bit much," she has said. "I find stepping back from my own life and thinking like someone else more interesting."

There are few writers from this part of the world, female or male, in Bakić's generation or before, who have cultivated an ear for speculative fiction, science fiction, fantasy, and the dystopian. Four in total, all men, come to mind: Bosnian Karim Zaimović, Croatian Davor Slamnig, and Serbs Zoran Živković and Borislav Pekić. Bakić's fusion of science fiction, feminism, eroticism, horror, and the macabre, is, indeed, unique within the literatures of the former Yugoslavia. In fact, Bakić has said that she, herself, was surprised to find how the stories took a speculative turn as this collection came together. Perhaps her university study of Bosnian literature and language in Tuzla offered Bakić models from which to depart, rather than models to follow.

She has also chosen not to write about the war. The Tuzla of her childhood was a dangerous and tragic place, the site of a May 1995 massacre of some seventy young people when she, too, was a teenager of thirteen, and hers was the town that sheltered the survivors, the traumatized women and children who fled the Srebrenica massacre in July of that same year. Of this she has said, "This is a part of my childhood from which I cannot escape: the shelling from Ozren and Majevica, the days without bread, power, and water, the wave of refugees from the Podrinje area. I don't write about it, but those are things I will never forget, just as I will never forget Yugoslavia, the only country in which I ever felt secure."

In his review of *Mars*, published on the website Booksa.hr in 2015, Dinko Kreho points out that the word "Mars" functions at three different levels for the reader of the Croatian edition: "Mars is, foremost, a mythical topos of science fiction and the popular imagination of the twentieth century, Earth's neighbor that inflamed the imagination of generations; Mars is also a key astrological symbol, the alleged 'male' planet juxtaposed to 'female' Venus. There is yet another dimension which Mars connotes for speakers of Croatian, having to do with the foreign, the alien, with not fitting in. *As if he came down from Mars* is said of someone who is visibly an outsider within a social setting or situation." Kreho makes the point that all three of these associations are present in Bakić's stories: her engagement with science fiction; her examination of gender relations and positions; and the ways in which individuals fail to fit into their social roles or constellation.

Asja Bakić strikes an eerie, Poe-like note in her stories, projecting dystopia through the lens of female sexuality. This mixing and mingling of genres recalls "weird" fiction in how she embraces the ghost story and other tales of the macabre. Writing and death are immediately linked for us in the first story, "Day Trip to Durmitor," and writing and death return again and again, singularly or in tandem through stories of grisly murders, corpses turning to lichen, writers facing their own clones. As an angel declares, "Literature is . . . the primary link between life and death."

The ordinary, understated way in which these stories narrate their extraordinary twists is what makes them leap off the page. In her translation, Jennifer Zoble follows the sudden shifts and quirks of the prose with a close and steady hand.

Each of these stories is different—some narrated in the first person, others with greater distance—but all have in common their inquisitive, exploratory protagonists who are trying to puzzle out, along with us readers, exactly what is going on in these worlds that don't, yet do, make sense.

—Ellen Elias-Bursać

ASJA BAKIĆ is a Bosnian author of poetry and prose, as well as a translator. She was selected as one of Literary Europe Live's New Voices from Europe 2017, and her writing has been translated into seven languages. She currently lives and works in Zagreb, Croatia.

JENNIFER ZOBLE is a writer, editor, educator, and literary translator. She coedits *In Translation*, the online journal of international literature at the *Brooklyn Rail*, and teaches in NYU's Liberal Studies program.

More Translated Literature
from the Feminist Press

August by Romina Paula,
translated by Jennifer Croft

La Bastarda by Trifonia Melibea Obono,
translated by Lawrence Schimel

Beijing Comrades by Bei Tong,
translated by Scott E. Myers

Chasing the King of Hearts by Hanna Krall,
translated by Philip Boehm

The Iliac Crest by Cristina Rivera Garza,
translated by Sarah Booker

The Naked Woman by Armonía Somers,
translated by Kit Maude

Pretty Things by Virginie Despentes,
translated by Emma Ramadan

The Restless by Gerty Dambury,
translated by Judith G. Miller

**Testo Junkie: Sex, Drugs, and Biopolitics in the
Pharmacopornographic Era** by Paul B. Preciado,
translated by Bruce Benderson

Thérèse and Isabelle by Violette Leduc,
translated by Sophie Lewis

Translation as Transhumance by Mireille Gansel,
translated by Ros Schwartz

Women Without Men by Shahrnush Parsipur,
translated by Faridoun Farrokh

The Feminist Press is a nonprofit educational organization founded to amplify feminist voices. FP publishes classic and new writing from around the world, creates cutting-edge programs, and elevates silenced and marginalized voices in order to support personal transformation and social justice for all people.

See our complete list of books at
feministpress.org